Kimberly Lang hid romance novels behind her textbooks in junior high, and even a Master's programme in English couldn't break her obsession with dashing heroes and happily ever after. A ballet dancer turned English teacher, Kimberly married an electrical engineer and turned her life into an ongoing episode of *When Dilbert Met Frasier*. She and her Darling Geek live in beautiful North Alabama, with their one Amazing Child—who, unfortunately, shows an aptitude for sports.

Visit Kimberly at www.booksbykimberly.com for the latest news—and don't forget to say hi while you're there!

THE PRIVILEGED
AND THE DAMNED

BY
KIMBERLY LANG

First published in Great Britain 2011
by Mills & Boon, an imprint of Harlequin (UK) Limited,
Eton House, 18-24 Paradise Road, Richmond, Surrey TW9 1SR

© Kimberly Kerr 2011

ISBN: 978 0 263 22027 8

Harlequin (UK) policy is to use papers that are natural, renewable and recyclable products and made from wood grown in sustainable forests. The logging and manufacturing process conform to the legal environmental regulations of the country of origin.

Printed and bound in Great Britain
by CPI Antony Rowe, Chippenham, Wiltshire

Also by Kimberly Lang:

THE GIRLS' GUIDE TO FLIRTING WITH DANGER
WHAT HAPPENS IN VEGAS…
BOARDROOM RIVALS, BEDROOM FIREWORKS!
MAGNATE'S MISTRESS…ACCIDENTALLY PREGNANT!
THE MILLIONAIRE'S MISBEHAVING MISTRESS
THE SECRET MISTRESS ARRANGEMENT

Did you know these are also available as eBooks?
Visit www.millsandboon.co.uk

To Jayk and Erica, who should really teach classes on how to raise awesome husbands. I can't thank you enough for mine.

CHAPTER ONE

GOOSE tossed his head and danced sideways, jerking Lily's attention back from her reverie just in time to see him angle her dangerously close to a low hanging branch. She ducked at the last second and steered him back to the path. "Behave yourself, you spoiled horse."

Goose merely snorted in response.

It would be her own fault if Goose's bad attitude unseated her. She knew better than to let her attention drift—Goose simply loved to challenge a rider and see who was really in charge—but the peace and beauty of the Marshall estate was hypnotic at times. When combined with the gentle cadence of Goose's walk as he cooled down from his run, it was hard not to let her mind drift away.

All those people who paid money for fancy yoga classes or time on a shrink's couch just needed to spend half an hour doing exactly this. They could quit twisting themselves into pretzels to meditate or digging up their daddy issues in search of peace. This was free therapy.

No, it was better than free; the Marshalls actually *paid* her. It was crazy, but true, and she thanked her lucky stars every single day that she'd landed here. It was perfect.

They were almost to the river, and Goose began to trot as the break in the trees grew closer. She could see the early-morning sunlight glinting off the water, and she turned her face up to the sky to let it warm her skin as they crossed the treeline. Goose walked straight to the water's edge and waded in, and only a sharp tug kept him from going directly to a depth guaranteed to soak her only pair of boots.

"Not this time, Goose. I'm on to your tricks. I'm not walking around with wet feet all day again."

As if he understood, Goose made a sound suspiciously like a disappointed huff, then lowered his head to drink. Pulling out her own water bottle, she took a moment to enjoy the view of the sun peeping over the mountains in the distance while she drank.

The Marshall estate—Hill Chase—was a little slice of heaven on earth. It was close enough to D.C. to allow easy escape and respite for the various family members immersed in politics and government, but it felt light years away from all that. It was also a business unto itself—as well as the family's home—and Lily did her best to just blend in with the scores of other employees. She took a deep breath of the clean air and blew it out, and the knowledge she'd been too cautious to really accept settled on her shoulders like the sunshine.

Her social worker had told her this day would come. Lily hadn't believed Jerry then, but now…

She really could start over. She already *had,* she corrected herself. The Lily she used to be was fading more and more every day, and the Lily she was now had finally begun to feel like the real her—like she'd been trapped inside a box and was just now able to freely move and breathe.

She shook her head to clear away the fanciful thoughts. While she'd be perfectly happy to spend all day right here, she still had two more horses that needed their exercise and a long list of other chores waiting for her at the stable. "Come on, Goose. Let's go."

"Already? You just got here."

Lily nearly jumped out of her skin at the voice, and her water bottle dropped out of her hand to land in the shallow water next to Goose's feet. She twisted sideways in the saddle to locate the owner of the voice and found a man swimming just a few yards away, only his head and shoulders visible above the water.

"Sorry. Didn't mean to scare you." The man's grin belied the apology.

"Just startled." That much was true. The estate was private, and no one knew she was here anyway, so she had no cause to be scared. Plus, as Goose's head jerked up he whinnied, seeming to recognize the voice. A second later the horse began to wade deeper toward the man, completely ignoring her scolds and attempts to stop him.

Thankfully, the man met them halfway, and she was able to tuck her feet up closer to the saddle and out of the water. Goose's big head lolled in pleasure as the man rubbed his nose, the reunion causing them both to ignore her for a moment.

And she needed that moment. The man was now close enough for her to recognize him: Ethan Marshall, one of Senator Marshall's many grandsons. She'd heard he was just back from an extended trip overseas—hell, the whole estate was abuzz with the news—and though she'd seen plenty of pictures, those pictures were nothing compared to reality.

All the Marshalls were genetically lucky—honey-blond hair, deep green eyes, strong jawlines under high cheekbones—but Ethan seemed to have won the lottery, combining those individual features into something more…more… Just *more*. Thick hair—curling just the slightest bit around his ears—dripped water onto broad, tanned shoulders. There, the droplets joined with others to run in rivulets over a set of lovely pecs and abs before meeting the water lapping his waist.

She jerked her eyes back up. *Mercy.* The man was gorgeous enough to give a girl heart palpitations, and when he looked up from Goose to meet her eyes and smile—seemingly aware she'd been checking him out, much to her mortification—the full effect was enough to cause her to sway in the saddle the tiniest bit.

"I'm Ethan Marshall."

"I know." *Eyes up. No gawking.* "It's nice to finally

meet you." She backed Goose up a bit, to relieve the strain on her thighs from holding her feet out of the water, but Ethan didn't follow. He looked at her expectantly and she searched for something else to say, but her brain was misfiring a bit now that she had his full attention. "Welcome back."

"Thanks. And you are…?"

Her cheeks heated. *Idiot.* "Lily. Lily Black."

"Well, it's nice to meet you, too, Lily. How many times did Goose soak your boots before you figured him out?"

"Three." He smirked, and she shrugged. "I'm a slow learner, I guess."

"Well, Tinker will do the same thing, too, if you didn't know that already."

Tinker was Ethan's horse, a huge white stallion with a mischievous streak worse than Goose's. "Tinker dumped me completely in the river on my second day." At Ethan's smile, she made the rest of the confession. "He then took off and left me to walk back to the stable."

Ethan laughed, a warm yet totally masculine sound that made her insides feel a bit gooey. "I heard about that. Didn't know it was *you,* though. Maybe I should apologize."

"Why?" His small shrug said a lot. "Did you *teach* him to do that?"

"It kept my brothers and cousins off my horse when I wasn't around." The unrepentant grin was slightly infectious and kept her at ease with the conversation. How long had it been since she'd had a friendly discussion about absolutely nothing at all? It was a nice feeling—even if it was a strange one, rusty from disuse.

"Your horse is rotten. It's a good thing he's pretty."

He winked at her, catching her totally off guard. "I've heard the same is said about me."

The statement could have been full of smug assurance of his good looks, but the tone made it sound self-deprecating. Unfortunately, it also had her eyes going back to the acres of tanned, sculpted skin. "Pretty" was a gross understatement of the man's very ample charms.

Goose was pulling against the reins, trying to move back out to the deeper water and Ethan, thankfully giving her something to concentrate on since she'd lost track of the conversation due to her wandering eyes. Goose snorted and shook his head, but she wasn't giving in. Not in front of Ethan Marshall. She didn't want him thinking she couldn't handle the horse.

"I think he's just happy to see you, Mr. Marshall. He's normally much better behaved with me."

"Ethan," he corrected. "Just Ethan. There are way too many Mr. Marshalls around here to keep up with."

Lily felt her face warm, but it wasn't with embarrassment this time. "Okay. Ethan it is." When he smiled this time, it caused a little shiver to run over her skin. That, along with the restless movements of Goose, brought her focus back where it belonged. "Um, I should probably get back to the stable. It was nice meeting you."

Ethan nodded. "And you, Lily."

She turned Goose back toward the shore and saw her water bottle in the shallows. "Mr. Marsh—I mean, Ethan—could you grab that bottle for me?"

"Nope."

She twisted around in the saddle to face him. The smirk on his face made her wonder if she'd totally misjudged him. It was a relatively simple request. Was his ego that big? A high-and-mighty Marshall was too good to retrieve a water bottle for one of the staff?

"I wouldn't normally ask, but I'm only wearing half-chaps, and if I get down my boots will fill with water."

Ethan shrugged a muscular shoulder. "Sorry. Can't be helped."

Maybe he *was* that smug after all.

The smirk grew worse as he crossed his arms over his chest. "I'm sure you didn't notice, but I'm only wearing water at the moment."

Lily felt her face heat again as the full meaning of his words filtered though. She'd been carrying on a conversation not six feet away from him—and he'd been *naked* the whole time? Her eyes—she just couldn't help it—retraced their earlier path down his chest and stomach to the waterline, which she now knew covered…

Ethan's chuckle caused her to jerk her head up and twist in the saddle so quickly her neck spasmed and Goose protested. "If I go get it, one of us could be embarrassed…" He trailed off, leaving no question as to which one of them it would be.

Oh, dear Lord. She was already embarrassed enough. Focusing her eyes on the shoreline, she saw a pile of clothes on one of the rocks. Dammit. *Why* couldn't she have noticed that just a little sooner? She'd been ogling the man's chest and stomach, and only inches below the waterline was… Her cheeks felt like they were on fire now.

"Still want me to get it?"

There was laughter and challenge in those words, and then she heard splashes, like Ethan might be making his way to shore after all.

"No!" She paused and cleared her throat. "I mean, never mind. I'll get it." Without looking at him, she dismounted, grabbed the bottle, and mounted again in record time. She dug her heels into Goose, feeling the water slosh around her toes, and set him into a trot. She didn't really care if it looked like the cowardly retreat it was; she had to get out of there before she died of embarrassment.

The sound of Ethan's laughter followed her, and it was all Lily could do not to kick Goose into a gallop.

Naked.

He'd been naked the whole time.

Distance from the scene of the crime helped her calm her heart-rate, but with that calm came unease. Ethan found it funny right now, but would he still find it amusing later on? What if he told others—like his grandmother? Mrs. Marshall wouldn't find it one bit funny.

Could she get fired for this? The thought chilled her. More than just the job, she loved—needed—the security of Hill Chase. It gave her a place to live and peace of mind. The thought of losing that because she'd been blinded by charm and a chest and not noticed he was skinny-dipping…

He was naked the whole time.

How will I ever be able to look him in the eye again?

Naked.

How could I have known?

It was an accident.

Lily lifted her chin. Exactly. An accident. No harm done. So the chances of losing her job were very, very low. She had to quit jumping straight to The Worst-Case Scenario all the time. The next time she saw Ethan—and it was guaranteed she would see him sooner rather than later, since the stable wasn't *that* big—she'd pretend it didn't happen. That would be the grown-up thing to do. Surely he'd like to forget the whole thing ever happened too.

So would she, but every time she closed her eyes she could see…

Nope. There would be no forgetting for her. Ethan Marshall wearing nothing but river water would be an image she'd take with her to her grave.

And, actually, she was really okay with that.

* * *

"Want to tell me what the hell that was all about?" Brady asked as he swung up onto Spider's back later that afternoon.

Ethan bit back a laugh as he checked the stirrups and mounted Tinker. Using his best innocent voice, he played dumb. "What was what about?"

"Lily tripping all over herself back at the stables and turning that amazing shade of red." Brady gave him that Big Brother look. "What did you do to her?"

"I've been here less than twelve hours. What makes you think I could 'do' anything to her?"

Brady snorted. "This is you we're talking about."

Lily's reaction when they'd walked into the stable had been almost comical. She'd taken one look at him, blushed the color of an overripe tomato, and nearly dropped the tack she carried. "Maybe she's always like that."

"I have to assume not, because she'd scare the horses otherwise."

"You assume? I thought you made a point of knowing everything about everything."

"I've barely spoken three words to her since she started working here."

Tinker and Spider walked slowly through the wide stable doors into the sunshine, and Ethan slid his sunglasses on against the glare. "Too good these days to talk to the hired help, are you?"

"Back off. It's not like I'm here all the time. I have a job, too, you know." Ethan heard the mild frustration and tiredness in Brady's voice. He was hip-deep in the political machine that practically defined their family—and had for more than forty years. Apparently it was wearing on him already. "She's barely spoken three words to me either. She's not the talkative type. Very shy."

Based on earlier today, Ethan would believe Lily was a little on the quiet side, but he wouldn't have guessed she was overly shy. Spider and Tinker were impatient and ready to run, but had to be held to a slower pace as he filled Brady in on their meeting in the river.

"And she didn't realize it?"

"Not until I told her."

"Oh, that's bad," Brady said through his laughter. "You really should have told her sooner. No wonder she's all flustered now."

"She'll get over it." When Brady didn't immediately agree, Ethan reined Tinker to a stop. "What?"

"Maybe you should apologize to her."

"For what? What did I do?"

"Besides not telling her you were skinny-dipping *sooner* in the conversation?"

"We're adults—"

"It doesn't matter. You're staying here for the next couple of weeks. That—" he tilted his head back in the direction of the stable "—can't continue. Give the girl a break. If you don't, you're a sadist every time you come to the stable."

Brady had a point. Although renovations should have

been finished a week ago, the workmen still had his condo ripped apart. Hill Chase would be his home base until they finished. And, while he doubted the work that had piled up in his absence would leave him much free time, he fully intended to make the most of any he managed to scrape out. He'd be around the stables a lot in the near future. If Lily was that flustered about their meeting, it would be cruel of him to let it continue.

Brady's phone rang and he fished it out of his pocket. A glance at the number had him rolling his eyes. "I have to take this."

Ethan nodded. Campaign season was about to go into full swing, and their father was in a hell of a fight to keep his Senate seat. Personally, Ethan didn't care if the current Senator Marshall kept his seat, but Granddad— whose Senate legacy was a plank in his son's platform, and probably the only reason Douglas Marshall had won in the first place—cared very deeply. And while Brady's sense of duty managed to outweigh his own feelings toward their father, Ethan's didn't. He couldn't bring himself to help his father, but out of respect for Granddad he managed not to hinder either.

But Brady, as one of the senior staffers, would be even more swamped than usual between now and the election. Ethan was actually surprised he'd gotten away today even for a short visit. Campaigns and politicking didn't take Sundays off.

Brady let his reins go slack, and Spider walked over to the side of the path to nibble on grass while Brady dealt with whatever the problem was. Tinker tugged on the reins, impatient to get going, but Ethan held him steady, waiting for Brady. He was home, finally, and happy just to be here. He wasn't in a real rush to get anywhere right now.

Over in the next paddock, he saw Lily leading Biscuit slowly by the halter. He hadn't known Biscuit had been injured, but the white wrapping on her foreleg and the slow, even pace Lily kept were clear indications the horse was on the mend from something.

Lily looked small standing next to Biscuit—he hadn't been able to truly tell her height this morning from her position on Goose's back. The dark green T-shirt with the "Marshall Stable" logo was a bit loose, almost camouflaging her curves, but she'd rolled the sleeves up over her shoulders, exposing nicely toned arms. The T-shirt was tucked into a pair of snug-fitting jeans that outlined the muscular thighs and calves he *had* noted earlier, before disappearing into the half-chaps.

Lily seemed to be talking to Biscuit, the action causing her long black ponytail to sway slightly, and Biscuit bobbed her head occasionally like she agreed with whatever Lily was saying. As if she felt the weight of his stare, Lily suddenly turned and looked over her shoulder, those black eyebrows disappearing behind her bangs when she saw him watching her.

Brady was still barking into his phone, and it sounded like he would be for at least a few more minutes, so

Ethan turned Tinker in Lily's direction. He could go ahead and get that apology out of the way.

Surprisingly, Lily met him at the fence. She looked up, shading her eyes against the sun, and though her cheeks looked a little pink, the earlier fluster was gone. Maybe the flush was from the heat.

"Is something wrong?" Concern showed in her big brown eyes as she looked over at Brady. "I thought y'all were going riding."

He dismounted. "We are. Brady's dealing with something at work right this second, so I came to apologize."

"Apologize? For what?" She seemed genuinely confused.

"For this morning—"

Lily shook her head. "I think I'm the one who owes you an apology. I'm terribly embarrassed—"

"So I gathered."

"I'd been trying to figure out how to apologize to you and then you walked in… Well, it caught me off guard." Lily wasn't quite meeting his eyes now.

"Well—" He was cut off as Tinker bumped him aside and nuzzled Lily's shoulder, catching her ponytail and tugging on it. "Hey!" He scolded the horse.

Lily smiled as she scratched Tinker between his eyes—his favorite spot. She knew his horse well, it seemed. "It's okay. You goofus," she murmured affectionately to the horse, flipping her hair back over her shoulder out of Tinker's reach.

Brady had pegged Lily wrong. She wasn't terribly shy, only quiet. Just like *he* thought. Since Brady hated to be wrong, Ethan couldn't wait to rub that in. He relaxed into the conversation. "I thought you said he was rotten."

"Oh, he is. To the core." Tinker was reveling in the attention, even butting Biscuit aside when she tried to horn in on Lily's affection.

"He certainly seems to like you. And Tinker doesn't like many people."

"He knows I'm a sucker for a charming pretty boy. We got off to a bad start that day at the river, but he won me over, and we get along just fine now. Don't we, boy?" she cooed at the horse.

"Then there's hope for me, too," he teased.

Lily froze for a second, then her brown eyes met his fully for the first time since that morning. A tug pulled at the corner of her mouth. "Are you comparing yourself to your horse?"

Oh, no, Lily wasn't shy, and that knowledge sparked something in him. He waggled his eyebrows in a leer. "In *many* ways."

Lily's mouth fell open at the innuendo, but she recovered quickly. "So the rumors *are* true…"

He cleared his throat, a tiny bit worried. "Rumors that…?"

"That *you're* a charming pretty boy, rotten to the core."

That caused him to smile. "Guilty as charged."

"At least you're honest about it."

"Honesty is important, don't you think?"

She paused briefly. "Usually."

How strange. "Only usually? Not always?"

The briefest of shadows crossed her face. He'd have missed it entirely if he weren't so focused on her. "Life's too complicated to draw lines like that. Sometimes a small lie is better than the truth."

"I'd have to disagree with you, Lily."

"Really?" She tilted her head sideways. "You believe in one-hundred percent honesty all the time?"

"Yep."

She scoffed. "That's not something I expected from you."

He stiffened automatically, but tried to keep his voice merely curious. "And why is that?"

"You *do* know your family's in politics, right?"

His loud bark of laughter had both horses looking at him in as much surprise as Lily. "Ergo my extreme desire for honesty above all else."

She laughed as well. "Then I'll keep that in mind."

Brady and Spider joined them at that moment. "Well, this is certainly an improvement from earlier."

Ethan could hear the tease in Brady's voice, but Lily flushed and her voice dropped anyway. "Sorry about that, Mr. Marshall." No wonder Brady thought she was painfully shy.

"No worries, Lily." Brady winked at her, and the spurt of anger Ethan felt surprised him. "I'm sure it was all Ethan's fault."

"Gee, thanks."

Brady shrugged. "Hey, the truth hurts sometimes."

Both he and Lily laughed, leaving Brady looking confused. Finally, he shook his head and gave up. "You ready, E?"

"Yep." He swung up on Tinker and adjusted the reins. "See you later, Lily."

"Have fun." She waved as they left.

Brady looked distracted as he kicked Spider into a trot.

Tinker automatically adjusted his speed to catch up. "Everything okay?"

Brady blew out his breath. "Just the usual messes. I'm going to have to head back tonight."

"Nana will be disappointed."

He shook his head. "Not as disappointed as she'll be if I don't go back to straighten this out and we lose this election."

"Maybe he needs to lose."

Brady sighed. "He's a lousy father, and a sorry excuse for a human being most days, but amazingly enough he's a damn good legislator. He learned *that* much from Granddad."

The contradiction didn't sit well with him. "Still, I don't know how you do it."

"I look at the bigger picture, Ethan."

"There's a bigger picture?"

"Yeah, it's called the greater good. Dad isn't afraid to

champion the tough issues or stand up for the little guy. He's doing good things, and I have to support that."

"I'll have to take your word for it."

Brady smirked. "Does that mean we can count on your vote?"

"Do you want the truth?"

Brady answered without looking at him. "Not really."

"Then I'll just keep my mouth shut."

"There's a first time for everything."

"Wow." Ethan put his hand on his chest in mock anguish. "Not feeling the love today."

"Like I said, there's a first time for everything. And it didn't look like it was from lack of trying, either."

"What's that supposed to mean?"

Brady's look was steady. "Lily," he challenged.

"You wanted me to apologize, and I did. End of story."

"If you say so." Brady's lips twitched. "You know, I never really noticed her before. She's quite cute. Nice legs. Shame I have to go back to the city tonight…"

Ethan knew when he was being needled, but it didn't counter the sudden unpleasant and completely irrational need to knock Brady off his horse. Brady's laugh only exacerbated that need. As if Brady read his mind, he dug his heels into Spider and the stallion leapt forward. Tinker reared up on his back legs, ready to go, and Ethan let him give chase.

It was good to be home.

* * *

Lily watched the two men banter as they rode away, the brotherly affection and annoyance obvious in equal parts. When Tinker took off in a gallop, her breath caught in her throat. Granted, the horse was beautiful, impressive, but the man on his back was far more so. Ethan looked like he'd been born in the saddle, moving easily with the horse and looking like some kind of centaur as he closed the gap between him and his brother easily. She could hear shouts and whinnies, and then the horses and their riders disappeared into the woods.

Over the past three months she'd figured out most of the Marshalls. They were a big family, with plenty of the private drama that came from the sheer number of them. There was also plenty of public drama—not unexpected, considering their wealth and power. Something always seemed to be swirling, whether it gave the tabloids their headlines or the eleven o'clock news its lead item or just had one or more Marshalls closeted in the former senator's study. They often fought amongst themselves, but they closed ranks and presented a unified front when attacked from the outside.

It was nice, yet odd at the same time. She really had no frame of reference to help make sense of it, either.

And now, just when she thought she was starting to figure it out, Ethan appeared on the scene, totally unlike what the rumors had led her to expect, and completely changing the energy she felt on the estate.

Energy radiated off him and made her tingle in unusual ways. And, while it still flustered her a little to have those green eyes on her, she had to secretly confess that the fluster wasn't all that bad a feeling. It made her feel... "Alive" wasn't the right word, but it was close.

Rumor had it that he would be staying on the estate for a while. Something about his place being refurbished and unable to be lived in. She'd probably be seeing more of him—she pushed back the mental image of the *more* she'd almost seen this morning—and the fact she didn't mind at all felt like a big step forward.

Too bad he had that whole thing about honesty.

CHAPTER TWO

THE growl of his stomach pulled Ethan's attention from the reports his assistant, Joyce, had emailed last week. The ones he'd pretended not to get. A glance out showed the estate was fully awake now, from the gardeners in Nana's roses under his window to the stable, where the horses were being turned out and the farrier's truck was pulling in.

Since the family as a whole and all its various members seemed to have remained financially solvent during his absence, nothing required his immediate intervention. He stretched, then closed the laptop and set it on the antique writing desk next to the window. The sun was shining—a very nice change from London's seemingly constant overcast skies—and there was no way he was going to waste the day closed up in his room.

The hall of the family wing was quiet now, but that could—and probably would—change at any moment. Hill Chase was the hub for their family, and everyone floated through here eventually. He'd even had an email from Finn this morning, claiming he'd fly in next week on his birthday for a visit now that Ethan was home. He'd wait to tell his grandparents, though, until his younger brother was actually in Virginia airspace, as there was a very good chance Finn would change his mind at the last minute.

He could smell coffee and fresh bacon as he came down the stairs, but once in the foyer he saw the light on in Granddad's study, and veered in that direction instead of the kitchen. The mahogany doors were open, and he could hear the clatter of a keyboard. Odd, since Granddad was practically a Luddite to begin with and, unless his arthritis had miraculously gotten better, typing at that speed was not possible for him.

Still, it was a bit of a shock to see Lily behind his grandfather's enormous desk, a pencil gripped in her teeth as she looked between the papers in front of her and the screen. Today, her hair hung in two braids down her back, and the effect made her look so innocent he was hit by a twinge of discomfort at the starring role she'd had in one of his dreams last night.

"Good morning," she said, the words a little distorted by the pencil. "I'm almost finished with these..." Another clatter and a click of the mouse and the printer hummed to life.

"Morning," he answered, and Lily jumped, turning sharply and catching the pencil as she spit it out.

"Ethan! I thought you were the Senator—I mean, your grandfather the Senator, not your father..."

"Well, I'm neither of them." He moved to the desk. "What are you doing?"

"Reports."

"And you don't have a computer in the stable office?"

Lily started to roll her eyes but caught herself. He stifled a laugh. Seemed he'd hit a bone of contention without even trying.

"Of course we do. It's just that the Senator…" She paused and bit her lip, like she was searching for the proper phrase. "Well, he's very particular in the way he likes certain things done."

"That's a nice way to say it."

"It's his stable. So I do it his way." She smiled slightly. "It's not that big of a hardship or anything." Pulling the papers from the printer, she stapled them and put them in a folder in the center of the blotter. Then she started gathering up her things and pushed the chair back. "But I'm done now, if you need the computer…"

"Nope. I just heard someone in here and came to see."

"Are you planning on taking Tinker out today? He's due to get new shoes, but I can make sure he's ready when you are."

"Maybe later. Don't worry about it, though."

"Okay. But call down to the stable if you change your mind." With her stack of file folders and ledger books and those braids, she looked like a student heading to class.

"How old are you?"

Her eyes widened. "I'm sorry, what?"

Nice move. "Never mind." He pointed to her coffee cup. "Need a refill? I'm headed to the kitchen myself."

"Um, okay. Thanks." She didn't move, though, and he must have looked at her oddly. "I'll have to follow you. I don't know how to get to the kitchen from here."

"Still learning your way around?" he asked as she fell into step beside him into the foyer.

"Kind of. I've only gone to the kitchen through the garden. Never from…" She trailed off and stopped, staring wide-eyed, and he looked around to see what the problem was. He didn't see anything.

"Lily?"

"Sorry, I've just never seen anything like it." Amazement filled her voice.

"Like what?"

"That staircase."

He looked, but all he saw was the marble staircase winding its way up like it always did. "Yes. It goes to the second floor."

She shot an exasperated look his way. "It's like something from a fairy-tale castle."

"Really?"

"Yeah. Like Cinderella could appear at any moment." She sounded so reverent he felt a little bad for teasing her.

He leaned closer. Lily smelled like fresh citrus, a clean scent that seemed to fit her perfectly. He inhaled again to enjoy it before he whispered, "Don't tell Nana, but right after those banisters get waxed you can pick up some real speed on the last turn."

"I bet—" the statement started out light, but became thicker as she turned her head toward him "—you c-can." She cleared her throat and stepped incrementally away, but not before he saw her eyes darken. Her tongue slipped out to moisten her bottom lip, and an arrow of heat shot through his stomach. She took another small step back and pasted a weak smile on her face. "Sorry for the delay. Lead on."

Right. He gave himself a strong mental shake, and they covered the rest of the distance to the kitchen in mildly uncomfortable silence.

As they got to the door, Lily picked up speed, pushing through with a chipper "Morning, Gloria. I bring you someone in need of feeding."

"Ethan! I was wondering when you'd come down." Gloria wrapped him in a hug that smelled like cinnamon and coffee before kissing him soundly on the cheek. "I'm sorry I wasn't here yesterday to welcome you home."

Gloria had ruled the kitchens at Hill Chase for as long as he could remember. She looked him over with a critical eye. "You've lost weight. Is there no food in London?"

"None like yours." Behind Gloria, he could see Lily refilling her mug from the carafe, smirking as Gloria clucked over him.

"Of course not," she said, preening. "Go sit and I'll fix you a plate." Without even looking over her shoulder, she added, "You too, Lily."

Lily froze in her attempted escape. "I've eaten already, Gloria. I just came for the coffee." She held up her mug and moved to the door. "So I'm going back to the stable now and will see everyone later."

Gloria sighed as she set an overflowing plate in front of him and filled his cup. "I swear, Lily's nothing but skin and bones."

As someone very appreciative of Lily's curves, Ethan would disagree with that statement. Silently, of course.

"That child doesn't eat enough to keep a cat alive," Gloria clucked.

Just the opening he needed. "Lily's hardly a child. She's what? Twenty-five?" he fished.

Gloria took the bait. "More like twenty-two or -three. She's just so sweet, though, it makes her seem even younger. And don't think I don't know what you're doing, either."

Ethan swallowed a mouthful of biscuit. "What?" he asked innocently.

"I'm wise to you. You leave Lily alone."

Lily had a champion already. "You make it sound like I'm planning on doing something terrible to her."

"Not on purpose, I know. But Lily's a good girl and doesn't need you messing with her head." Gloria pursed her lips. "Or her anything else, for that matter."

"I was simply curious as to how old Lily was. Now I know." He vaguely wondered what Gloria knew that had her so protective of Lily. Even from him. "Is there more sausage?" he asked to change the subject.

Predictably, Gloria's need to feed took over and she immediately went to the stove. "I'm afraid you're on your own today. The Senator and Mrs. Marshall left early this morning to go to the Weatherlys' to see the new foal Spider sired. It was planned before they knew you were coming, but they knew you'd probably have plenty to keep you occupied."

He did have plenty to do: a ton of emails waiting for his attention, and a dozen phone calls he should make. But they'd waited this long; another day wasn't going to make that much of a difference. A whole day of doing nothing important sounded very appealing. "No problem. I'm sure I can find something to amuse myself."

Gloria slid the sausage onto his plate and frowned at him. "And never in your life has that sentence not equaled trouble."

Lily knew the moment Ethan entered the stable. The energy felt different. It sounded just as silly today as it had yesterday, but she would swear it was true.

Maybe it was just because she happened to be mucking the stall next to Tinker's when the horse perked up and started whinnying.

In twenty-four hours she'd managed to develop quite a crush on Ethan Marshall. It was silly, to be honest, but true nonetheless. After all, what *wasn't* crush-worthy about the man? As long as she accepted it for exactly what it was, then there was no harm in it. She was a realist; she knew how the world worked and her place on the food chain. It was no different, really, than a crush on some movie star equally unobtainable.

Still, though, it felt rather nice; just another emotion she hadn't let herself experience in a long time.

She heard Ethan greet his horse, and the way he talked to Tinker made her smile. These horses were family pets—not for competition or show—and as far as she knew there wasn't a Marshall in the bloodline who wasn't completely horse-crazy.

Screwing the lid back on the bottle of motor oil, she stepped out of Duke's stall, drawing Ethan's attention and a lazy smile of greeting that made her stomach flutter a little. Then the bottle caught his attention. "Duke's cribbing again?"

"Yeah. I swear that horse needs therapy. Or antidepressants. Nothing we're doing seems to help, so I'm trying to at least make his stall taste bad before he chews it to bits."

"Finn says he's coming out next weekend. Maybe that will help settle Duke down."

Finn, she knew, was Ethan's younger brother. The wild one who lived out in Los Angeles and produced movies—whatever that entailed. "Couldn't hurt. Maybe Duke just misses him." Tinker was butting against the stall door, wanting out. She patted his nose. "You are next for new shoes, so stay put." Realizing that Ethan probably wanted to ride, she added, "Sorry. We're a bit behind. Things are a little crazy around here today."

"When are they not?"

"Very true." She put the oil bottle on the ground and picked up the stall pick. Going back into Duke's stall got Ethan out of her line of sight and let her stomach settle.

She started spreading the clean bedding over the floor. "If you want, I can call up to the house when Tinker's ready," she said over her shoulder.

"It's not a problem."

Ethan spoke from right behind her, causing her to jump. She turned, surprised he'd followed her in, only to get confused when she saw the pitchfork in his hand. "Um…" Surprise and confusion turned to complete jaw-dropping amazement when he started banking the bedding into the corners like a pro. "Um, what are you doing?"

Ethan looked at her like she was a little slow.

"I mean, I know *what* you're doing. What I want know is *why* you're doing it." *In here.*

"You said things are crazy today, and I thought I'd help."

Ethan Marshall. Mucking a stall. Two things that did *not* go nicely together in her head. "What if you get caught doing my job—"

"Honey, I've mucked these stalls thousands of times."

"Really?" She was too distracted by the movement of his powerful shoulders as they forked another load of bedding to say much more.

"Yes, really." He shot her a grin. "In fact, I'm probably better at it than you are."

Like that was something Ethan would put on his résumé. "I'll take your word for it, honestly." Confusion reigned, and Lily struggled to make sense of the scene before her. "Look, if you're waiting for Tinker—"

"It'll do me some good. I spend too much time behind a desk these days. I'm getting soft."

"Soft" was definitely not one of the many adjectives she'd choose to describe Ethan. Biceps strained against the fabric of his T-shirt as he worked, thigh muscles contracted and flexed under faded denim that hugged a *really* nice, tight... Lily moved to stand in front of the fan and closed her eyes as the air rushed over her face.

"You okay?" She looked over to see Ethan had stopped working and was now watching her, eyebrows pulled together in concern.

"I'm fine." She poked at the bedding with her pick, moving it around aimlessly, unable to really focus.

"The summer I was fifteen, the stable manager's niece came to work here. She might have been older than me, but she was the most beautiful girl I'd ever seen." He leaned on the pitchfork. "She knew it, too, and told me how impressed she was by my mucking technique. I mucked more stalls that summer..."

"To impress her?" *Because good looks, charm and money weren't enough?* The girl had to be crazy. She couldn't imagine a teenage Ethan would be lacking in any of those attributes any more than he was now.

He laughed ruefully. "She just wanted someone else to do the work, but, yeah, I thought I was impressing the hell out of her every day."

Could she get fired for letting Ethan do her job? That was something she really couldn't afford to risk. "If I tell you I'm impressed, will you stop?"

"You don't want help?"

"Really not. I'd prefer to do it myself."

Ethan looked at her strangely, but set the fork aside. "Then be my guest."

Lily breathed a small sigh of relief. "Thank you." Maybe her crush on Ethan wasn't as good an idea as she'd convinced herself. She was making an utter ass of herself.

Instead of leaving, however, he leaned against the wall, like he had all the time in the world and no place better to go. She tried to pretend he wasn't there and just finish up, but Ethan was simply impossible to ignore. Tinker stuck his head over the wall and nuzzled against his shoulder, and he lifted his hand to pat the horse absently. "So, where are you from?"

Damn. It was a perfectly innocent question, but she still hated it. It was a gateway to more questions. "Mississippi."

"That explains your accent. What part?"

She tried to sound nonchalant, shrugging and falling back on practiced answers. "We moved around a lot, so nowhere particular."

"What brought you to Virginia?"

It was as far as I could get before the money ran out. Swallowing against the curl of nausea, she struggled this time to keep her voice light. "A desire to see a different part of the country."

"It must be tough to be so far from your family, though."

She bit back the snort. *He* might see it that way. "Can't be helped, so I'm dealing with it."

"Gloria says you took the apartment over the office."

Focus on what you're doing. Maybe he'll get the hint. "Uh-huh."

"And do you like living here at Hill Chase?"

She could hear the teasing impatience in his voice at her distracted, vague answers, but she was getting impatient to end this conversation. "Not to be rude, but can I ask why you're asking all these questions?"

His eyebrows went up in surprise, and she regretted the sharpness of the question. "Being friendly?"

There's friendly and then there's freaking me out. "Why?"

"Maybe I'm just a friendly guy. Is that a problem?"

Yeah. "I realize we got off to a weird start, but please don't feel like you have to be nice to me or anything. I just work here."

Ethan was silent for a moment. Maybe she'd gone a little too far. He finally nodded. "Then I'll leave you to it."

"Thank you." Lily grabbed the empty wheelbarrow and rolled it away, feeling Ethan's stare on her back as she left. Once outside, she parked the wheelbarrow by the wall and sagged against the building.

She'd just been horribly rude to her boss's grandson, but she couldn't help it. Why, exactly, she didn't know. It wasn't like no one had ever asked her those questions before. They were simple enough conversation, nothing really out of the ordinary, and until now she'd been able to fake her way through. There was something about having Ethan ask her, though, that made it harder.

Clarity arrived a little too late, and she banged her head against the wall gently. Her little crush wasn't harmless at all.

Thank God Ethan wouldn't be staying long at Hill Chase this time. She'd just have to make her way through it as best she could. And by his next visit she'd have it—hell, everything—better under control.

Ethan watched Lily turn the corner, the tension in her shoulders so fierce it had to be painful. She was acting like a few simple questions were the equivalent of the Spanish Inquisition. He looked at Tinker. "What is Lily's deal?" The horse rolled his eyes. "You don't know either, huh?"

However, anyone who thought Lily was shy was blind and possibly stupid. That much he knew for sure now. Lily simply didn't want to talk, and that was a far cry from being shy. He fully understood the feeling; he'd just never been on the receiving end before.

The correct thing to do would be to leave Lily alone, respect her privacy, and forget the way those big brown eyes moved over him like a breeder evaluating a stud.

That last bit was unlikely, since just the memory was enough to make his skin burn. And that made the chance of him doing the other two "correct" things also rather slim.

More importantly, he didn't want to. Something about Lily's fresh-faced earthiness intrigued him. Unlike the over-polished women from the country club Nana kept pushing at him, Lily seemed real. And, unlike the women who wanted him for his name or his money or his status, Lily acted like those were marks *against* him. Lily was different and she posed a challenge—two things he suddenly, and oddly, found irresistible.

His phone vibrated in his pocket as a text came in.

Need you to make an appearance at fundraiser Saturday. Black tie.

Not likely, he thought, and deleted the message.

As if Brady knew what he'd done, a second message appeared.

The Grands will kill you if you don't show.

Boy, Brady was really pulling out the big guns. First some lecture on the "greater good" to appeal to his sense of reason, and when that didn't work going back for the bigger ammunition of Nana and Granddad. He suddenly felt the need to visit Finn in California on Saturday. No one expected Finn to play nice, to put on the happy family face for the donors and the voters, and Ethan envied that. At the same time, things had been much harder for Finn: he'd been too young to understand what was really going on, and his and Brady's attempts to shield Finn had only made things worse in the long run. As far as dirty laundry went, it wasn't enough to derail the campaign in any way, so while it wouldn't serve any purpose ever to air it, it still galled him to play along.

He deleted Brady's second message and put the phone

away. Ignoring the unpleasant, pretending it didn't exist, putting a positive face on… That was just the Marshall family way.

And he was, as everyone liked to remind him, a Marshall.

But at the same time…

He pulled his phone back out and sent Brady a short message: *No*.

Two hours later, Lily felt like the biggest idiot on the planet. But not because of her little crush. She could deal with that. It was embarrassing, but not shameful. And it was the shame driving her feelings of idiocy right now.

She'd overreacted. Taken everything in the wrong context. Let her own feelings and fears color what, in retrospect, was obviously completely innocent. Ethan, it seemed, really was just a friendly guy. While Tinker was off getting shod, he wandered around the stable, talking to everyone from Ray, the stable manager, to the guy delivering feed, and pitching in to help with whatever that person was doing at the time. At one point she walked around a corner—thinking he had left already—only to find him amusing the barn cats with a frayed piece of rope.

Quite the idiot, indeed. And now the mental self-flagellation was giving her a headache. To make the whole thing even worse, a glance at the clock said it was only just past two. This ridiculous day was barely half over. She needed aspirin.

The fact a room came with the job had been a big plus when she'd applied, and was even more so today. A couple of minutes alone would help the headache as well as give her a chance to regroup.

But it seemed this day wasn't finished messing with her head just yet, because *of course* she had to run right into the cause of her headache. Dammit, the Marshall estate was practically the size of her hometown— why did she have to see him every time she turned around?

Lily attempted what she hoped was a casual, non-committal yet friendly nod as she passed, but when Ethan returned it the quirk of his lips had her picking up her pace, mounting the stairs and climbing them two at a time. Honestly, she didn't care what he thought.

Halfway up, she missed a step. She grabbed for the handrail, but didn't quite manage to stop her fall.

Her foot went through the riser space, sending pain shooting up her leg as the wood stair dug into her shin and her knee twisted. Falling sideways, she saw stars as her head banged the handrail.

A second later she felt hands on her shoulders, steadying her, and she was able to catch her breath. She knew without looking who her savior was. *This day couldn't possibly get any worse.*

But then Ethan was tilting her chin up, his eyes scanning her face for damage, and she had to rethink that idea. "You okay?"

"Yeah. Just clumsy." Embarrassment combined with close proximity to Ethan had her face feeling sunburned.

He helped her untangle her leg and pulled her gently to her feet. She winced as she put weight on her leg, and Ethan frowned. "Let's get you inside and assess the damage."

"I'm fine," she protested, only to end up sputtering as Ethan bent slightly and hooked an arm under her legs. A second later she was cradled against that chest she'd been admiring yesterday—and it felt even better than it looked. She inhaled, liking the simple smells of sunshine and man and soap, allowing herself to enjoy this feeling for just a brief moment. Her skin heated, but she wasn't sure if that was her or the warmth of his skin seeping through his shirt.

He climbed the remaining stairs easily, as if she weighed nothing, and turned sideways to carry her into the apartment. As he eased her down onto the bed, moving pillows behind her so she could lie back against the headboard comfortably, Lily felt her heartbeat stutter.

"Just a bang. It's fine." Granted, she did feel a little addled, but it had nothing to do with hitting her head. In fact, she was starting to get used to the feeling.

Ethan crossed to the little kitchenette in two steps, and Lily realized how tiny her apartment really was. He seemed to fill the entire space, making it feel even smaller. Returning a second later with a wet paper towel, he dabbed at a place above her eyebrow, and the stab of pain surprised her.

The hissing sound she made caused him to frown.

He fished in his pocket and produced a cell phone. "I'm calling a doctor."

"That's not necessary. I'm okay. Just a little banged up. No big deal."

Ethan didn't seem convinced, but he put the phone away. "We'll see. Do you have any ice packs?"

"Not up here."

"I'll go down to the office and get some, and a couple of bandages, too." The ease with which Ethan took charge was oddly comforting. "Do you need help getting your jeans off?"

Shock cut through her. "Excuse me?"

"We need to look at your leg too."

Lily looked down and saw blood seeping through the fabric over her shin. Suddenly the throbbing pain intensified. "I can handle it."

"Then I'll help with your boots." Before she even processed what he was doing, or could form a protest, her cropped boots were off and Ethan was almost out the door. "I'll be back in a second."

She was still reeling in various stages and kinds of shock, but she had no doubt he'd be back in no time. Ethan seemed to want to play knight in shining armor at the moment. And, while she wasn't exactly the average damsel in distress, she had to admit it was kind of nice to be fussed over a little.

Especially by Ethan.

That didn't mean she wanted Ethan's help removing her clothes, though, and she shimmied out of her jeans as quickly as she could, wincing as the denim peeled away from a raw-looking scrape that nearly covered her entire shin. This was the last straw: even if she had to give up eating, she was buying new boots with her next paycheck. Tall ones. She was tired of wet feet and banged shins...

The sound of feet on the stairs brought her back from her mental grumble, making her realize that she was nearly naked to the waist and that her T-shirt barely reached the tops of her thighs. She reached under the pillow for her pajamas and slid the short bottoms on just as Ethan opened the door.

He carried cold packs from the freezer, and the stable's bright red first aid kit. Her heartbeat kicked back up again. Maybe she *had* hit her head harder than she thought... He dropped the red bag on the bed next to her. "Towels?"

She pointed to the closet.

He was efficient and oddly professional as he wrapped a cold pack in a small towel and indicated she should use it on her head. Another towel went beneath her leg before he produced a bottle of saline from the first aid kit. "This might sting a little," he warned.

"You don't have to—*ouch!*"

"Wimp," he teased, and grinned at the dirty look she shot him. "How's the head? Any blurriness or double vision?"

"Nope." She pulled the towel away from her forehead and noticed the blood on it. "Boy, I'm really a mess. I don't need stitches, do I?"

"It's just a nasty scrape. Keep the ice on it. Anything else hurt?" Ethan dabbed at her shin with gauze.

"That does," she gritted out. "Look, I'm okay—really. I appreciate the help, but I can take care of it."

He waggled his eyebrows. "And give up the chance to fondle your leg? No way."

It was such an odd, out-of-place comment that the absurdity of it made her laugh out loud. Ethan grinned. She sat back against the pillows and put the ice pack on her forehead. She wasn't concussed, and she wasn't imagining things. Ethan was actually flirting with her. In the privacy of her apartment. While she wasn't really wearing all that much…

Maybe he was just the kind of guy who flirted with every woman who crossed his path. Maybe it was just part of that whole "being friendly" thing. She really shouldn't read anything into it—after all, hadn't she already made that mistake once today already? It was still fun, though—except for the blood and pain part.

Her ego was enjoying it enough, however, to scrape the rust off her own flirting skills. "Do you fondle all the stablegirls' legs?"

"Only if they're bleeding." He grinned as he worked. "I don't want to get slapped, you know."

"Good policy." She examined the bandage on her shin as he taped it into place. "I'm impressed."

"So am I." He shot her a sideways smile. "You've got great legs. Very fondleable."

If her heart beat much faster, she'd pass out. Maybe she

wasn't quite ready to scrape *all* the rust off those skills just yet. "I meant the bandage. Very nicely done."

"I have many talents."

I'll bet, she thought, before she squashed it.

Ethan tidied up after himself and carried the trash to the can. "You'll probably want to take some aspirin or something. Your head—and everything else—is going to start hurting soon. Do you have any?"

"I do." She started to slide her legs off the bed, only to have Ethan stop her.

"Just sit for a minute, okay? You nearly gave me a heart attack out there."

"Maybe you should be the one resting, then," she mumbled. Ethan looked at her expectantly. "Fine. In the bathroom. Medicine cabinet."

He nodded and went to get it. She heard the cabinet door open, and the thought of Ethan riffling through her private items bothered her. Then he was back, fixing her a glass of water and handing her two tablets.

He leaned a hip against her table and watched while she swallowed the pills obediently. "Thank you, Ethan. I'm not normally so accident-prone. But I do appreciate the save. And the bandaging."

"Does that mean I'm forgiven for whatever I said this morning that ticked you off?"

He really didn't shy away from the direct questions, did he? "I think I'm the one who owes you an apology. Again." She tried to laugh it off, but it was hard to do so with Ethan staring at her. "I guess I'm not what you'd call a 'people person.' I need to just stick with the animals. Speaking of which, I should probably get back to work."

"I think you should take it easy for a while."

"Nah, I'm fine." She removed the ice pack from her head and touched the sore spot with her other hand. Her fingers came back clean. "The bleeding seems to have stopped."

"Well, quit touching it. Here." Ethan dug through the first aid kit and pulled out a Band-Aid. He sat next to her again on the bed and leaned across her to inspect the cut. "You'll probably have a bruise tomorrow, but I doubt it will leave a scar."

Lily heard the words, but they weren't making a lot of sense. Ethan was really, *really* close, and all of the oxygen in the room seemed to disappear. She tried to inhale, but only got a lungful of his unique scent that sent shivers through her racing bloodstream.

She closed her eyes and tried to calm her pulse. *Bad idea.* Without visual distraction she felt his touch more keenly. His fingers were gentle as they smoothed over her forehead, but the skin felt scorched.

"Am I hurting you?"

Her eyes flew open; a big mistake because now Ethan's attention was focused on *her,* not her injuries.

And he was still really, *really* close. Close enough for her to see the tiny flecks of gold in the green of his irises and count each of his eyelashes. Now she really couldn't breathe, and she felt light-headed.

Time froze as his eyes darkened and moved slowly over her face. Her heart was in her throat, and a warm, melting feeling oozed through her chest. Ethan was only inches from her; she could feel his breath against her lips already, and the trail of his fingers from her injury to her chin was a feather-light touch, hypnotic and paralyzing.

Then his mouth met hers. A soft, slow, barely-there touch that teased her, making her lips heat and tingle. His thumb slid along her jaw and down her neck, and the melting feeling in her chest developed sharp edges of want.

It was those sharp edges that focused her. Weakly, she put her hand on his and felt the tension there. *He was holding back.* She dragged air into her lungs painfully. "Wh-what are you doing?"

His chuckle was the sexiest thing she'd ever heard, rolling over her skin like a caress.

"Kissing you." Ethan punctuated the statement with a slide of his tongue against her bottom lip. "Unless you want me to stop…"

No! Every nerve-ending in her body screamed in unison, nearly—but not quite—drowning out the alarm bells in her head. Ethan's other hand slid to the pulse at the base of her throat. *Focus.* She closed her eyes. "But…*why?*"

CHAPTER THREE

THAT was a damn fine question, and for the life of him Ethan couldn't come up with an answer better than "Because I want to."

He heard Lily's gasp in response, and the pulse in her neck fluttered under his fingers. She must've liked that answer. "B-but do you think it's a good idea?" she whispered.

"Best one I've had in a long time." He pressed another kiss against the corner of her mouth and felt the tiny shiver that ran over her skin. "You taste delicious, Lily."

"Oh." The muscles in her neck relaxed, giving him access to the soft skin under her jaw. The hand holding his slid to his wrist and her fingers tightened. Her chin dipped, and Lily's lips met his—hesitantly at first, then gradually more insistent. Her tongue touching his was spark to the powder, igniting a fire in his stomach that raced through his veins.

Lily angled her body toward his as she sank into the pillows, and the kiss grew deeper, hotter, more devouring. One hand held his wrist tight as he traced over a delicate collarbone and moved lower to rest on her chest, right over her pounding heart. When her other hand gripped his bicep it was icy-cold and the contact against his heated skin…

Cold? His brain was tangled from Lily's kiss, but the small part still working knew that wasn't right. Icy…ice pack…*injury.*

He smothered a curse as he pulled away. Lily looked confused. *And delightful,* his half-stunned brain added, but he forced himself to focus. He was pawing an injured woman just moments after patching her up. Lily didn't seem to mind, but still…not his best moment.

"Ethan?" She bit her bottom lip—still swollen and moist from his kisses—and her forehead creased in confusion. The movement must have hurt her head, because the crease smoothed out and she lifted a hand to rub around the bandage. "Is something wrong?"

One of her braids was loose now, but he had no memory of releasing it—only of how silky it had felt between his fingers. Her breathing was still slightly erratic, and pink tinted her cheeks. When Lily licked her lips and pushed her hair out of her face with a shaking hand it was all he could do not to reach for her again. He cleared his throat and ran a hand over his face—noting he wasn't exactly steady either. "Nothing's wrong, but you should probably rest for a while. I'll tell Ray what happened and have him come check on you later."

Lily looked…shocked? Disappointed? Upset? It was

hard to tell because she dropped her head and her hair fell across her face.

"Take it easy, okay? And keep the ice packs on." She nodded and he stepped outside. Shaking his head to clear it, he questioned his sanity a bit.

He didn't regret kissing her—not by a long shot, he thought ruefully, and tried to calm his body down a bit—but Lily's "good idea" question did have merit. Now that he *wasn't* kissing her, at least.

There were the obvious problems—the fact she worked for the Grands was a huge one, actually. Nana and Granddad disapproved of any kind of not-strictly-professional relationship with the staff. It was a good way to either get slapped with a sexual harassment suit or make the front page of the tabloids. Or both.

Plus Lily was young and very sweet. She might not be able to understand or handle the ground rules he always made sure to lay down—ground rules that should have been established *before* he kissed her in the first place.

None of this rational self-talk could take the sharp edge off the desire still knifing through him, though, and he rubbed a hand across his stomach. Lily was a sinful temptation, and now that he knew she tasted as sweet as she looked...

Tinker was probably back from getting his new shoes and ready to ride, but there was no way he could sit a saddle in his current condition. Maybe his best bet would be to head back to the main house and work awhile before dinner.

First stop, though, would be a shower. A very cold one.

Dinner could have been an uncomfortable affair, except that Nana had a hard and fast rule about unpleasant topics at her table. Douglas Marshall was definitely an unpleasant topic—at least for Ethan. So they talked *around* the elephant in the room, keeping the conversation safely on the horses, politics in general, Ethan's trip to London, and Nana's latest charity project.

But once the coffee was cleared away Nana retired with a claim of fatigue, and Granddad suggested they move to the study—a sign that he was probably about to be called on the carpet, exactly as Brady had predicted.

Hell, it wouldn't be the first time. Or the last.

Granddad's study was a moment frozen in time—all dark woods and old-world elegance. His aesthetic dislike of "new" kept this room firmly entrenched in the past: the only nod to this century was the computer on Granddad's desk, and that was only because Granddad couldn't figure out a way to either not have one or camouflage it better. But the study was comforting in its familiarity and lack of change.

Granddad went directly to the bar, poured two Scotches and handed him one.

"You're not supposed to drink that," Ethan chided, as he took his glass and leaned against the fireplace.

"So that's what you were doing with yourself in London for so long. However did you find the time between partying and making the tabloids to finish a medical degree?" Granddad lowered himself into a chair facing the cold hearth and stretched his legs as he took a sip out of his glass. "If I want advice we have plenty of doctors in the family already, though."

"And you're obviously not listening to any of them." But the Scotch was excellent, and Granddad wasn't one to give up his pleasures without a fight.

"What your grandmother doesn't know won't hurt her. Or me." Granddad raised a white eyebrow at him in challenge. "Are you planning to tell on me?"

"Possibly."

Granddad shook his head. "Not fond of your trust fund, are you?"

Ethan smirked. "Just don't drink all of it, okay?"

"Son, I'm old, and I've earned this drink. Life isn't worth living without a few small pleasures." He took a sip and closed his eyes briefly in enjoyment of the liquor. When he opened his eyes a second later, the stare nearly pinned Ethan to the mantel. "So, are you ready to just cut to the chase?"

"Might as well." *Get it over with.*

"This is going to be a tough election. Mack Taylor wants that seat. All the incumbents are in for a hard fight, and we are no exception."

We. Like they were all up for election, not just his

father. The idea of a "family business" took on new meaning when the business was politics.

"I've been keeping up. The poll numbers are still good—"

"But not great. Taylor likes to run dirty, mud-filled, negative campaigns, so those numbers are very volatile. We could be down before we know it."

"Dad is running on your name and your legacy. Hell, half the voters think they're still voting for *you*."

"Just something else Taylor seeks to change. We need all hands on deck, and that includes you. Starting with the fundraiser."

"I'm busy that night."

"Then un-busy yourself. I don't expect you to actively campaign, but I do expect you to show up and smile."

"Sorry. I'm not a hypocrite."

"But you *are* a member of this family, and therefore you have a vested interest in seeing that we continue to hold this seat."

"I'll take my chances."

"You can't. The Marshall family rises and falls together." Ethan started to rebut that, but Granddad stayed him with a hand. "You have a responsibility not only to this family, but to the people of Virginia and the rest of the country. You can't just shrug that off."

Granddad liked to play both the duty and the responsibility cards, and as hard as Ethan tried it was too ingrained in him to ignore. He sighed and took the opposite seat. "Here's the thing…"

"I'm not unaware of the 'thing,' Ethan, and that's

why I don't ask more of you." His voice was quiet and earnest. "I'm not always proud of the man Douglas is. As his father, that's a hard truth to swallow, because it's my failing. The way he treated your mother was shameful, and you boys deserved much better than he gave. You still do. I have to wonder where I went wrong with your father."

Granddad was a career politician, but this was the most honest pain Ethan had ever heard. For the first time ever Granddad looked old. Tired.

"But I am proud of the man you are. Finn and Brady, too. Keeping this seat is more than just protecting my legacy. It's protecting yours, too. Dirty laundry creates a stink that covers everyone and never really washes away. What we present to the public protects us all from that stink."

"That's dishonest."

"No, that's politics. People like to think they're electing someone they like—someone like them, or someone they'd like to be. But the best person for a dirty job isn't always the one you'd want to have a beer with after work."

Hadn't Brady said pretty much the same thing? "Like Dad."

"Like your dad." Granddad sighed and swallowed the last of his drink. "Look at it this way—I won't have to ask you again for at least six years."

Ethan knew when to give it up, no matter how much it galled him to do so. It still *felt* dishonest, even though he wasn't really lying to anyone. Dad was a good senator, and would probably do more good things in his next term. He was splitting hairs, but as long as no one expected him to endorse anything other than his father's legislative record he wasn't actually *being* dishonest. "Fine. Fundraisers and general party activities. I can do that. But that's all."

Granddad nodded, and the tired look etched into his face disappeared. Ethan could soothe any residual angst with the knowledge that at least he'd made Granddad happy. He didn't owe his father anything, but he did owe Granddad everything.

"That's actually good, son. Keep the focus on the issues, because that's where we're strongest." Pushing to his feet, Granddad reached for Ethan's empty glass. "I'm having another small splash. Care for one?"

Did he ever. Ethan handed over his glass gratefully.

Lily had wandered through her day, unable to shake off the bemused fog. Or maybe it was a confused fog. Either way, she was having a hard time concentrating. She wished she could chalk the fog up to a slight concussion, but she knew she hadn't hit her head all *that* hard. No, the fuzzy-brained feeling had Ethan Marshall written all over it.

More specifically, Ethan Marshall's kiss.

Even now, hours later, she was still sighing over it like a teenage girl. As far as kisses in general went, Ethan got high marks for quality. Hell, her toes were *still* curled up in pleasure. And when he'd found a sensitive spot on her neck she hadn't even known existed... *Damn*. It made the muscles in her thighs clench just remembering.

Like she could forget it. Lily was having a hard time convincing herself that it had really happened and wasn't just some fantastical daydream kicked up by a knock to the head. Maybe it was some kind of reverse amnesia—instead of forgetting things, she was remembering things that didn't actually happen.

If so, it was one hell of a nice and real-feeling daydream. She could still feel the weight of his mouth, the tension humming through him. She could still *taste* him. And she'd never had a daydream of any sort with that level of detail.

Ethan Marshall had kissed her. That idea was just so ridiculous, though. Things like that just didn't happen to someone like her. People like the Marshalls kissed people like them: rich, well-connected, well-bred, well-educated...

She was none of those things. And it wasn't like Ethan didn't know that. She worked in his family's stables, for God's sake. It wouldn't take a huge assumptive leap on his part to know she wasn't in his social circle. Maybe in a movie some princess or socialite might hide out in the working class, but this was real life.

She was a Mississippi redneck who lived paycheck-to-paycheck. The only connections she had were to the kind of people who made shady, back-alley, cash-only deals and ended up on episodes of *COPS* wearing handcuffs. His father was a senator; her father was a felon.

His family tree boasted governors and CEOs; hers had nothing but shine-runners and horse-thieves.

Oh, and there was that small issue of her own record...

Yeah, the Ethan Marshalls of the world didn't kiss folks like Lily Black. At least not on purpose. Or more than once.

Which explained why Ethan had beat a fast retreat out of her apartment earlier. He must have realized what he was doing. It wasn't a kiss she was likely to ever forget, but she certainly wouldn't hold her breath for it ever happening again.

It had been a weird, weird couple of days.

Which might explain her inability to sit still for longer than a minute or two and why she was wandering through the stables at eight o'clock in the evening instead of curling up on her bed with some mindless television.

The stables were pretty quiet, and it wasn't like the horses needed to be checked on or anything, but it gave her something to do with her restlessness...

Tinker's stall was empty, the door standing open. Lily looked around, half expecting to see Tinker wandering through the stable, looking for a snack, but no horse. *Damn.*

Her heart skipped a beat before she calmed herself down. Tinker was a valuable horse, but not one someone would steal—and Tinker was ornery enough to not go willingly with a stranger. Even if someone had accidentally left his stall open—and if someone had, that would get them fired—Tinker was too spoiled to stray far from the comfort of home. So where the hell was that horse?

Remain calm until there's a reason to panic or sound the alarm. Lily went to check the paddock and, sure enough, as soon as she stepped outside she heard hoof-beats. A second later her heart skipped a beat for an entirely different reason.

Ethan was riding Tinker. Bareback. They looked like something from a movie, silhouetted against the trees with the moonlight throwing Ethan's features in and out of shadow. *That* was definitely a sight to make a girl sigh. Especially one who was still in the afterglow of his kiss and nursing a massive crush. She could happily lean here against the fence all night and just watch.

But Ethan must have noticed her, and Tinker trotted to the fence a moment later. "You're out here late, Lily."

Act casual. She was just glad it was dark out here and the flush in her cheeks wouldn't be quite so noticeable. "Don't let me interrupt. I was just looking for Tinker since he wasn't in his stall."

Ethan patted the horse's neck. "I never did get to ride today, so…"

"Then I'll leave you to it." She pushed off the fence. "Goodnight, Ethan."

"Lily—"

"Yes?" *Please don't mention earlier. I don't want to hear that it was a mistake. Let me keep that memory just as is.*

"Would you like to come along?" Ethan extended a hand to her, and she realized he meant on Tinker. With him. Just like in some movie.

All that rationalizing from earlier nagged at her. All of those very valid reasons telling her to say goodnight again and go back to her apartment. But her brain and her blood weren't exactly in agreement. Would it really hurt anything if she said yes?

Hadn't this been what she'd been working toward? Well, not this *exactly*—this was outside the realm of even her daydreams—but something like this? A fresh start in a new place where no one knew of her past? Where she had nothing to try to live down or up to? For once being accepted just for herself, without anything clouding the issue?

Hadn't she *earned* this? A reward of sorts?

It didn't help that Ethan looked like something fresh from a fantasy himself—hair mussed, a slight five o'clock shadow emphasizing his jawline, controlling the stallion just with a set of reins and really nice thigh muscles.

She didn't know when she'd regressed to a moony fifteen-year-old, but the quivery feeling in her stomach and the heat surging through her veins were not signs of maturity.

Then Ethan smiled at her, and she really didn't care anymore. She slipped between the fence rails and let him help her climb on.

Riding bareback was a completely different experi-ence from using a saddle. She could feel the heat of the horse seeping through her jeans immediately—but then she was pressed against Ethan's back, and the heat was even more intense. She had no choice but to wrap her arms around his waist—not that she didn't love the excuse—and the hard muscles there brought back the still-vivid picture she had of those muscles covered in nothing but a few drops of water.

Her head didn't clear his shoulder, keeping her from seeing where they were going, and her nose and lungs were filled with the Ethan-scent she remembered from earlier today.

The force of so many sensations slamming into her at once had her feeling light-headed. Ethan opening the paddock gate barely registered, but his, "Hang on!" did. He waited until her arms tightened before nudging Tinker, and the stallion took off.

It was exhilarating—like nothing else she'd ever experienced. The estate was draped in shadows, and those shadows whipped by at a dizzying speed as they headed toward the river. The dark and the quiet made Lily feel like she and Ethan were the only people for miles. It was easy to just relax into the motion of man and horse, let the wind cool her cheeks and tug at her braid, and enjoy the rush of adrenaline.

Ethan slowed Tinker as they approached the river, cooling him down, and Lily was finally able to catch her breath. "Wow. That was amazing. I've never felt anything like it." *That's not entirely true,* her brain argued as Ethan chuckled and those abs moved under her hands.

"Have you never ridden bareback before?" Ethan turned his head slightly toward her as he spoke, putting his mouth just inches from hers.

"No. I don't ride the horses for fun, remember?"

"Pity. You did great, though. Definitely a natural."

Tinker stopped at the water's edge, and Ethan held out his arm to help her slide off. He followed, then let Tinker wander down to the water for a drink. Lily's surprise must've shown on her face. "He won't go far, and he'll come back."

"How interesting. If I did that, Tinker would be half-way back to the stable by now."

"Because Tinker knows who's the boss. And it's not you." He winked at her. "Sorry."

"He should try to remember who feeds him, though, and have a little respect for that," she grumbled.

A fallen tree made a sort of bench, and Lily took advantage of it, since her legs still weren't entirely stable. It was a quiet, beautiful, moonlit night, but suddenly a bit discomfiting. She was a long way from the stable, alone in a romantic setting with a man who made her insides melt *and* who had already kissed her once today.

The hope he would do it again battled with the fear that he actually might. When Ethan joined her on the log, she tensed involuntarily.

"Don't worry, Lily. I'm not going to pounce on you. In fact, maybe I should apologize for earlier."

"Oh." *Damn.* No! *Good.*

He sat quietly for a moment. "Or maybe I should apologize for later."

Now her brain really was twisted into knots. "Why?"

Ethan didn't look at her. Instead he leaned back against the tree trunk and cushioned his head on his arms. "Because I'm thinking I'll do it again before we go back."

Lily didn't know if she should laugh or pull her hair out, but her heart was pounding again. "Is that a prom—?" She caught herself in time. "A warning?"

His eyes were closed, but a small smile tugged at the corners of his mouth. "Just a prediction."

"I see." Breathing was a whole different issue, though. She was very glad he kept his eyes closed. When he didn't say anything else, Lily realized Ethan was giving her the chance to object, to turn him down, but she couldn't bring herself to do it. Regardless of how smart it would be to do just that. "It's a nice night."

"Indeed."

She pulled her feet up and wrapped her arms around her knees. "Is that why you decided to go for a ride? Because it's a nice night?"

"That, and the fact that I really had to get away from the house for a while."

The frustration in his voice caught her off guard. "Why is that?"

There was that little smile again. "For someone who doesn't like to answer questions, you sure do ask a lot of them."

"I do?"

Ethan smirked, and she realized what she'd done.

"I mean, I guess that's true. I just think other people are far more interesting. I know *my* story already."

Ethan finally opened his eyes. "But I don't. Know your story, that is."

"You're not missing much." That wasn't *entirely* true, but it wasn't a lie either. "Why do you think I left Mississippi?"

"If you're looking for adventure, Hill Chase isn't the right place to find it. There's not much excitement to be found."

She rested her chin on her knees and studied the river. "I'm not looking for adventure or excitement. Just something else. Something other than what I had. Haven't you ever wished to…?" She realized whom she was talking to. "No, I guess you haven't."

"Haven't what?"

"Wanted to go somewhere where no one knew you and had no preconceived notions or expectations."

"What makes you think I haven't? Or that I don't wish that every single day?"

She turned to face him. "Because… Because you're…" *Handsome, charming, rich, powerful.* "A Marshall."

He laughed dryly. "You say that like it means something special."

"It *does*," she stressed.

Ethan snorted.

"You mean it doesn't?"

"It means that everyone gets sick of their life occasionally, Lily. *Everyone* wants to run away from home at some point."

"Hmm."

An eyebrow went up. "Just 'hmm'? No 'why' this time?"

She was more than a little amazed at how easy it could be to talk to Ethan. "Oh, I'm dying to ask why, but then I'd feel honor-bound to answer *your* 'why' questions, and I don't think we're ready to be confidantes. Or that we ever should be. It would be inappropriate, considering I work for your grandparents."

"Interesting way to look at it."

"Just less complicated." *In many ways.*

He sat forward and rested his elbows on his knees. "I get the feeling you don't like complicated."

"I prefer simple. It's easier."

"That's too bad."

"Why?"

"Because things are about to get complicated anyway."

That was all the warning she got. Ethan had gotten so close during their conversation that he only had to move a couple of inches and his mouth was on hers.

Oh, *yes.* Her earlier arguments posted a brief protest to her rational self, only to be quickly shouted down. Who gave a damn about maturity and rationality, anyway? This wasn't an experience she was likely to get to repeat, so she'd be a fool to let it go to waste.

She was many things, but a fool wasn't one of them.

Ethan's kiss wasn't like any kiss she'd ever had

before—hungry, yet patient; teasing, but full of all kinds of dark, wicked promises and possibilities.

And those promises and possibilities intrigued her.

Ethan shifted, pulling her fully into his lap and settling her so that her legs crossed his lap as he leaned back against the tree trunk. One hand moved to the small of her back, and she felt his fingers curl through the belt loops at her waist—like she was tempted to go *anywhere* at this point. The other had pulled her close to his chest.

If there was a more perfect moment in time, in a more perfect setting, Lily didn't know what it could be. But the feel of Ethan's lips on her neck, the strong bulk of him under her thighs…the moonlight, the sound of the river… It had to be real, because her imagination wasn't *that* good.

Her palms tingled as she smoothed her hands over the soft cotton that separated his skin from her touch. The hidden ridges and valleys fascinated her, and she traced them with her thumbs, pleased by the way the muscles contracted and his heartbeat thumped in response.

Ethan tugged her shirt out of her jeans and those hands were hot against her back, then her ribs, before finally snaking up to cover her breast. She gasped at the bolt of heat that shot through her.

The gasp caught Ethan's attention. He hadn't been kidding earlier when he said he planned to kiss her again, but pawing the woman hadn't been on his agenda. Her taste, the way she responded… Lily was a drug that snatched away his common sense. And his control.

Another minute and he'd have her on her back on the hard ground.

Her eyes widened as he told her just that. *"Oh."* The word was a sigh, tinged with disappointment—a feeling he shared, because he was not prepared for the possibility.

A second later she slid off his lap and stood. She tucked in her shirt and smoothed her hair, effectively ending the moment and any possibilities with efficient movements designed to put space between them.

Her sharp whistle had Tinker trotting over, much to Ethan's surprise. Lily took hold of his bridle. "I should probably go back now. Could you drop me off before you finish your ride?"

The words were clipped, showing her discomfort regardless of how casual she tried to act. Even in the moonlight he could see the flush climbing her neck and staining her cheeks again.

Once again he was in no condition to ride—in a condition he was beginning to wonder might become permanent whenever Lily was around. But he climbed aboard Tinker anyway, searched for the least uncomfortable position, then helped Lily up.

He felt her hesitate before she grasped his waist. Before, she'd molded herself to him: breasts heavy against his back, thighs snuggled up behind his. This time she tried to keep space between them, her hands light and her body stiffly held away.

Risk of discomfort or not, he was tempted to let Tinker take off at full speed, which would force her to either get close or get thrown off. Instead, he let Tinker meander his way in the direction of the stable.

Attempts at idle conversation were met with vague, nearly monosyllabic answers that only got worse as they neared the building.

"Lily, look—"

But Lily was already sliding off ungracefully. "Thanks for the ride," she said, backing away toward the stairs. "Goodnight." She spun and took the stairs two at a time, just asking for another fall.

She never looked back, never broke stride as she opened the door and disappeared inside.

And he didn't have a clue what *any* of that was about.

CHAPTER FOUR

A VERY restless, nearly sleepless night left Lily feeling like a zombie the next morning, and all the coffee in the world couldn't help. But it wasn't just the lack of sleep clouding her brain; no, once again she had Ethan to thank for that.

He was a contradiction that had her brain misfiring in confusion. While his actions seemed to indicate Ethan was interested in her, she couldn't think of one good reason why he *should* be. But she couldn't help but be flattered. And excited. Even though she knew she shouldn't be anywhere near Ethan, it hadn't kept her from crawling into his lap last night.

And she'd been so swept up in the sensations and the moment… She took a deep breath and stamped down the memories that seemed equally imprinted in her mind and her skin. She was just very lucky he'd come to his senses when he had.

Ethan was so far out of her league they weren't even playing the same game. And, while she'd enjoyed flirting with the possibilities, last night proved beyond any doubt that she was definitely not ready to move up from the minor league.

"Lily, honey, I think it's clean enough now." Ray's voice cut into her thoughts. "I appreciate your attention to detail, though."

Lily looked down at the bridle she'd been cleaning for who knew how long, then gave the stable manager a sheepish smile. "Sorry. I'm not all here today."

"Is your head okay?"

Her head was a total mess, but Ray probably wasn't asking about *that*, and she nodded. "I've got a small bruise, but that's it. The leg's a bit sore, though." Both legs were sore, and her thighs had been screaming at her this morning for riding bareback last night, but she didn't offer up that tidbit of info.

"If you need to take it easy today..."

"No, I'm fine," she assured him. "Just the change in the weather making me daydreamy. I love fall."

Ray nodded, and Lily went back to cleaning tack, forcing herself to concentrate on the task at hand, not who she'd had her hands on last night.

It didn't quite work.

Some days, it just wasn't worth getting out of bed. Four measly hours into this day and it already sucked. Fed up with just about everything, Ethan closed his laptop before he started sending emails he'd regret later. He took a deep breath to calm his rising anger. He should probably put the phone off-limits too.

It was a point of pride for him—realizing he was

reaching the end of his tether before he got there. Although he had his father's temper—had inherited it in spades—*he* knew how to control it. Or at least how to not let it control him.

And now would be an excellent time to take a break. Honestly, Joyce was more than just an assistant, and could easily handle most of this herself without his input or assistance. In fact she was a financial wizard, with the ability to juggle multiple million-dollar balls and never drop a penny, and she'd probably appreciate not having Ethan butt in. But Granddad insisted on having family in charge of the family business. And, while there were plenty of Marshalls to choose from, the number who were willing or able to be tapped for the jobs was distressingly small.

Just another thing to cause his blood pressure to rise. Carefully and deliberately, he pushed his chair back from the desk, putting physical distance between him and his computer.

Of course, part of his current black mood had a lot to do with the fact he'd woken up grouchy and frustrated. And while that was Lily's fault, he really could only blame himself. It wasn't like she had any control over the things she'd done in his dreams again last night.

He needed to deal with that situation today as well. The thought helped his blood pressure greatly, if for no other reason than it sent all his blood rushing to his lap.

Ethan was tempted to head to the stable now, but

common sense told him Lily would be working. Like he should be.

There was that black cloud again.

Gloria's voice over the intercom, letting him know lunch was ready, was a welcome distraction from the conflicting moods caused by work and thoughts of Lily. His grandparents were already seated at the table in the small family dining room by the time he arrived.

"There you are, dear. I haven't seen you all morning."

Ethan paused to press a kiss against Nana's cheek. "Unfortunately I've had a ton of work to do."

"It's not healthy to stay locked in an office all day," she scolded. "I did hope you'd be spending more time out of doors in the sunshine and fresh air. We won't have this gorgeous weather for much longer."

As far as Nana was concerned he was still about fourteen. Sometimes it was sweet, especially when she patted his cheek like that. "Trust me, I can think of several things I'd rather have spent my morning doing." *That was an understatement.* "But duty calls."

Granddad laid his fork down. "Speaking of calls, I got one from Sylvia today."

He'd already had his blood pressure spike over that today. "So did I, Granddad. It's taken care of."

"Good to hear. She did say that she's been trying to get in touch with you for days."

"Aunt Syl thinks everything is an emergency. And, honestly, I refuse to be lectured about my business responsibilities by a woman who has never worked a day in her life." Ethan caught the small smile on Nana's lips as she cut into a tomato. The relationship between Nana and Aunt Syl was complicated and full of mutual annoyances.

"Oh, I heard about that, too," Granddad grumbled.

"Why am I not surprised?" He shrugged. "The truth hurts sometimes."

Nana pinned him with one of those looks guaranteed to make him feel like a child again. "But there are *ways* to be truthful and yet tactful at the same time."

"I don't have time to dance around Aunt Syl's feelings. If she'd just been patient..."

"Not everyone appreciates your bluntness, dear."

"Then they need to find someone else to talk to."

"Ethan..." Nana seemed ready to launch into one of her favorite lectures.

"But when I bluntly tell you how lovely you look today, you know it's an honest compliment, not just bull—" He caught Nana's frown and corrected himself. "Empty flattery."

Nana shot him a look that said she wasn't buying it, but she did drop the subject.

"However," Granddad cut in, "Sylvia will be at the fundraiser Saturday, and you'll need to behave yourself. I smoothed her feathers today—took me forever, too—so don't go ruffling them again."

Just another reason why Ethan liked to avoid those events: too much smiling and nodding and shallow pretending. At least if he put in an appearance at this one he'd have a better chance of begging off the next time.

But he nodded, accepting Granddad's edict, and both the Grands seemed pleased.

"Oh, and by the way," Nana added casually—too casually *not* to get Ethan's attention. "Senator Kingston's daughter is back from Europe as well, and she will be there Saturday night. She's such a lovely girl. You know, her grandmother and I were just talking about…"

That statement, coming fresh on the heels of Nana's lecture on tact, was no coincidence. Nana was old, but she was still sharp. She also wanted great-grandchildren.

He looked at the mountain of food on his plate. Sadly, lunch was a long way from over.

Shower. Dinner. Sleep. In that order. Lily had made it through the day, but just barely. She had no doubt she'd sleep tonight—she just had to stay awake long enough to wash the smell of horses off her and eat a bite of something.

As she climbed the stairs to her apartment a huge yawn caused her jaw to crack, and she figured she'd be willing to forgo eating. It wouldn't be the first time she'd gone to bed without dinner, so she knew she'd survive.

The hot water felt divine, as did clean pajamas, and both revived her enough to cause her stomach to growl. She made a quick sandwich and turned on the news.

They were interviewing Senator Marshall—the current one, Ethan's father—and he looked so much like Ethan her heart skipped a beat. Basic looks, though, was as far as the father-son similarities went. Douglas

Marshall was articulate and passionate about the issues, but he left her oddly cold. Maybe it was because she knew the generations above and below his.

Personality-wise, Ethan was more like his grandfather, whom she adored. She'd never met either of *her* grandfathers, but she liked to pretend they'd be a bit like Porter Marshall—as unlikely as that could possibly be. The older Marshall had a friendly approachability about him that must have skipped a generation.

Douglas was just too slick, and his charm seemed forced instead of natural. Lily knew he was a good senator, but he didn't seem like a good *man*. She had nothing at all to base that on beyond a gut feeling, but she'd been trusting that gut feeling her entire life, and it had never let her down.

It might be an unfair judgment, since he wasn't as horsy as the rest of the family and didn't come down to the stables much when he visited the estate. She hadn't had the opportunity to interact with him much at all, but self-protection had no use for "fair" when it came down to it.

Douglas Marshall reminded her of Pop—only with power and money to back him. It made her skin crawl, and she felt a little sorry for Ethan and his brothers.

Vaguely she recalled something Ray said about Ethan and his brothers living here on the estate after their mother died. That would help explain why Ethan was so close to his grandparents, and why he was more like the former Senator than the current one. She was also cynical enough to wonder why they hadn't remained in the primary custody of their father.

There was always a reason for that.

Or maybe not, she argued with herself. Maybe she was reading things through her own non-rose-colored glasses again. Maybe the rich and powerful did things differently than the rest of the world.

She'd still lay her bet that it had more to do with Douglas Marshall than anything else.

But it was none of her damn business. She shouldn't speculate. And she turned the TV off as she finished her sandwich and reached for a book instead.

Three pages in, she remembered what she'd forgotten to do today in her zombie-brained state, and she cursed. The feed order had to be in by eight, and a glance at the clock showed her she had ten minutes. *Just enough time.*

Lily slid her bare feet into her boots and pulled a hoodie off the hook behind the door. She looked ridiculous, but she wasn't in a fashion show. On the off-chance she did run into someone in the stable this late, the pajamas covered everything important. She grabbed her keys and went downstairs to the office.

The computer took forever to boot, and Lily drummed her fingers impatiently, one eye on the clock.

The ordering itself was easy, and she'd done it dozens of times now, but it still took time to do. Hitting "send," she checked the computer's clock. Two minutes to spare.

"Yes!" she crowed. "I rock."

"Forgot the feed order, huh?"

Lily nearly jumped out of her skin at the voice; the voice's owner registered a half a second later, and she spun in the chair to see Ethan leaning against the office doorframe. "Not entirely—because it's done. With time to spare, I might add."

Once again Ethan seemed to fill the room more than was normal, making her feel like there wasn't enough oxygen for them both. His body also blocked the only exit, which was nerve-racking for a reason that had nothing to do with fear. And, while there was a desk between them to act as a barrier, Lily was suddenly very aware of how little clothing she actually had on.

And that she lacked underwear.

She tugged the edges of the hoodie closer to each other. "Are you going riding again tonight?"

"Hadn't planned on it. Why? Would you like to go?"

"Oh, no—thanks." Ethan still didn't move. "Is there something you needed in here, then?"

"No."

Oh, she was not in the mood to play Twenty Questions right now. "Then you're here because…?"

"You weren't upstairs and the lights were on in here."

It took a minute for the words to process. "You were looking for me?"

He nodded. "Yep."

She was very glad he'd found her here and not in her apartment. *This* was bad enough. "I'd ask why, but I'm not sure I want to know," she muttered.

Ethan's lips twitched in amusement. "I came to talk."

That was what she was afraid of. "About yester-day…?"

"Yeah, let's talk about yesterday."

She took a deep breath. "We can just forget it happened. No problem."

Ethan's eyebrows went up. "Try *big* problem."

"I don't want to lose my job."

Ethan stepped inside and closed the door behind him. "And I don't want to be accused of sexual harassment."

"I don't want this to get all complicated and awkward and messy."

"Neither do I."

They were agreeing this wasn't a good idea. Why, then, was Ethan still looking at her like that? "Then why can't we just forget it happened?"

"Because I don't want to. I probably *should,* but I rarely do what I should."

Lily knew that feeling, that freedom. It almost always led to bad decision-making. And sometimes jail-time. It was also a very hard habit to break. "So you always do what you want?"

"Usually. Unless it's impossible."

"So what do you want from me?"

Surprise crossed Ethan's face. "*From* you? Nothing."

Her heart sank a little. That honesty thing of Ethan's could be a real pain.

He crossed the office in a heartbeat and rounded the desk. Placing his hands on the arms of her chair, he caged her as he leaned forward until their faces were only inches apart. "I just want you."

On second thought, that honesty thing might not be so bad. Four words had never done quite so much for her libido. The room felt very warm all of a sudden, and her lack of underwear no longer seemed like a problem. She swallowed hard.

There could be repercussions. It could prove to be a bad decision. She just might regret this.

Or not, she corrected as Ethan kissed her. She locked her arms around his neck and let him lift her from her seat. He backed her against the desk and she boosted herself up onto the surface, allowing him to fit nicely between her legs.

The kiss turned carnal then, wild and devouring. Ethan slipped the hoodie down her arms and off, and his hands found the bare skin of her back under her pajama top, pulling her even closer to his body.

She wanted to feel *his* skin under *her* hands, and his shirt frustrated her. She tugged impatiently at the hem, sliding it up until Ethan finally lifted his arms and allowed her to pull it up and off. Then he did the same with hers.

Lily wanted to be pressed against his chest again, wanted skin-against-skin contact, but Ethan traced a finger over her collarbone and down between her breasts. His scrutiny had her feeling extremely self-conscious, but the look on his face made her think he might be pleased with what he saw.

Ray kept a pile of old saddle blankets in the office,

and Ethan scooped one up in one hand as he tightened the other arm around her waist and lifted her off the desk.

When Ethan lowered her to the floor on top of the blanket, Lily had a small moment of panic. *Moment of truth.* Time to put up or shut up. But it all felt so good—and strangely right—and all rational arguments were quickly shouted down by the feel of Ethan's hot mouth on her breast.

With the embers still smoldering from last night, that touch was all it took to light her blood on fire. A hand slid over her stomach, spreading the heat down to her hip, then the curve of her thigh. His fingers teased under the hem of her pajama shorts, then slid inside to wrap around a cheek as his mouth caught hers again.

She didn't know what felt better—his hands on her, his mouth against her neck, or his skin against hers. His skin was hot under her palms as she explored, feeling the thump of his heart against his chest and the contractions of the muscles in his stomach when she traced them.

Ethan's kiss was hungry, his hands demanding, but he wasn't hurried. The slow slide of her shorts down her legs was followed by a leisurely exploration on his way back up—carefully avoiding the bandage on her shin—and her skin trembled in its wake.

She was naked; Ethan wasn't. She wanted to change that. Now. Her hands were shaking with desire as she reached for the clasp of his jeans and found him straining against the zipper. She ran her hand over the bulge, and Ethan returned the pressure with his hips as he groaned into her mouth.

She felt like an electric current was thrumming through her body, causing shocks and tingles like she'd never felt before. She felt clumsy and ham-handed as she struggled with his zipper, and finally Ethan moved in to help her. He removed the last of his clothing with ease, never letting the task interrupt the play of his lips and tongue, and Lily realized she really was way out of her league in more ways than she'd wanted to think about.

She flattened a hand against his chest, putting a few inches of space between them, and gasped for air as she broke the kiss. "Th-there's something you should—you need to know."

It took a second for Lily's words to filter into his brain and make sense. That sentence didn't bode well at any time, but at a moment like this, and the tense way she said it… Her face was flushed, her breathing ragged, and she couldn't meet his eyes as she chewed at her bottom lip.

He tilted her chin up and caught her eye. "What?"

"I, um…" She blew out her breath. "I don't do this often."

He had to turn that one over in his head for a minute, looking for the meaning, but the deepening color in Lily's cheeks finally gave it to him. "Often? Or—" *God help him* "—never?"

"Often." She laughed nervously, and he tried not to let his relief show. "I just…didn't want you to get your… your expectations up too high."

It was a vulnerability he hadn't expected Lily to possess, much less admit to. And, while her words implied some hesitation, her hands were still busy, caressing him eagerly. He chose his next words carefully. "I didn't have many—but you've already exceeded them all."

That earned him a smile, and Lily threaded her fingers through his hair, pulling him back to her. The kiss was drugging, instantly addictive. He could happily feed on her for days, but not touching her more would kill him very quickly.

Lily's body was a study in contrasts—silky skin draped over muscles toned by real work, not a gym membership. The different shades of her skin, from the freckles across her nose to the fair skin of her stomach, came from working outside in the sun, and he ran his tongue over the paler skin that contrasted against the tan on her shoulder. When he tasted her, short, blunt fingernails dug into his shoulders—a practical necessity that contrasted with the impractical bright pink color he discovered on her toes.

Everything about Lily was *real,* something sorely lacking in the rest of his life. It was refreshing and very, very arousing.

Lily's hesitant confession pounded through his mind, reminding him to go slowly and carefully, but her response to his touch fired his blood and stole much of his ability to think. The need to bury himself in her—to feel that silky hot skin wrapped completely around him—took over.

Ethan reached for his jeans with one hand, searching the pocket until he found the condom he'd optimistically stashed there earlier. Lily moved restlessly beside him, encouraging him to hurry, then sighing when he rolled her beneath him.

Lily couldn't hold a thought for longer than a second. Her body burned and ached at the same time, and while she wasn't sure how much more she could stand, she didn't want Ethan to stop touching her. Ever.

The weight of him between her thighs was bliss; the slow slide inside her body...torture. She was stretched to the brink, but craved more, pressing her hips up to meet his. She could feel the strain of his muscles—the strength and power and the desire held in check—under her fingers.

Just when she thought she'd go insane from the waiting Ethan began to move, and she no longer cared about her sanity. Each thrust pushed her higher, until the pleasure became too much to bear and tremors shook her body. She held on to Ethan as he took her over the edge. Someplace in the distance she heard Ethan's growl and felt the arms holding her shake.

And then everything exploded.

Ethan looked slightly smug as he trailed a finger lightly down her arm. Lily wanted to smack him on principle, but she really couldn't muster the energy to move. And, anyway, he'd certainly *earned* the right to look smug. Hell, her vision was still gray and fuzzy around the edges.

"You okay?" he asked. There was humor in his voice, and he dropped a kiss on her shoulder.

Her lips didn't seem to be functioning properly either, as it was tough to form a response. Not that her brain could come up with one anyway. Lily settled for a smile and a slight nod. She closed her eyes again.

"I'm sorry if I hurt you."

Her eyes flew open, and she saw the concern on his face. *Ugh. She shouldn't have even brought it up.* "I told you, I wasn't a—"

She could tell Ethan was biting back a laugh. "I meant your leg. And your head." He traced a finger around the Band-Aid on her forehead.

"Oh." *How humiliating.* "No. Both fine."

"Good." Then all humor disappeared, and his eyes narrowed a little. "But…um…if it…"

Kill me now. "All good. Really."

An eyebrow went up. "Just 'good'? I really do owe you an apology, then." He reached for her hand and lifted a finger to his lips, allowing it to trace the lazy, sexy smile there. "I was aiming for 'amazing.' Maybe even 'fantastic.'"

"Fishing for compliments?" *Because "fantastic" doesn't even come close.*

"Well, I hate to think I buckled under the pressure." He nipped at her fingertip, and it caused a shiver to run through her. "I'm sure I'll do better next time."

Her mouth went dry. "Next time?"

"*This* time," he corrected as he rolled her beneath him again.

CHAPTER FIVE

A REGULAR day off had been hard for Lily to adjust to. The rest of her work schedule might change from week to week, and her irregular hours might be considered odd to most people, but Wednesdays were always hers. The first couple of weeks she'd wandered around, unsure what to do with herself, but now she had a routine, she found herself looking forward to the time.

The thirty-minute drive back to civilization used to feel like an eternity, but she was used to it now. Liked it, even, because she liked the seclusion of Hill Chase, and the distance to town just reinforced the feeling of being far from it all.

As always, her first stop was the bank to cash her paycheck, then the Laundromat, where the owner greeted her and offered to change over her loads while Lily took care of her other errands. The next stop was the drugstore to pick up a few toiletries. The average mindlessness of it all was slowly becoming her new normal.

Just something else she was coming to love.

Today, though, her wander through the drugstore

came to an abrupt stop in front of the condom display. Like she wasn't having a hard enough time keeping her mind from wandering back to last night...this just brought it all vividly to the forefront of her mind.

Her face heated, but it wasn't regret or shame. Last night had been the stuff of fantasies, and she had no regrets at all. She'd still been sighing into the wee hours of the morning as sleep refused to come. But the bright light of day had her facing the reality she'd let herself ignore last night.

Crush or no crush, fantastic sex or not, she'd be a fool to read anything into what had happened. Ethan had been pretty clear about his intentions—simply by *not* making claims or avowals or romanticizing—and she respected that.

And, honestly, she wasn't sure she *wanted* a lot of talk and explanation and all that. Sometimes you just had to grab the moments of happiness and not question where they came from or why. It made things much simpler.

She didn't regret sleeping with Ethan—not at all. Physically, it was the best sex she'd ever had. Not that she had much to compare it to, but she certainly couldn't imagine it getting any better. Although Ethan had asked—vaguely, at least—she hadn't been able to give him fully satisfactory answers about why she, at the age of twenty-two, had less experience than most would expect from a woman her age in this century.

How could she explain—without confessing more than she wanted to—that even a delinquent like her had realized at some inner level that there were pieces of her soul she just didn't want to give away?

Why sleeping with Ethan was different was a puzzle to ponder another day. She just needed to accept it for what it was and enjoy the memory. There was no need to plan on any repeats either. Lily turned her back on the display and went to the register before she could change her mind.

Her face was still feeling hot as she returned her books at the library and checked out the new ones Judith was holding for her behind the desk. Then she went to one of the computers and checked her email account.

Only a few people had the address. She'd wanted— *needed*—to make the break as clean as possible, but there were a couple of people she wanted to keep up with, however infrequently.

Seeing TJ's return address made her smile. TJ's transition out of the halfway house and back into real life had been rocky, but she seemed to be getting it together now. Her last email had been full of excited news about a new job and a new boyfriend. A "respectable" one this time, TJ had insisted.

When she opened the message, though, it was brief.

He's looking for you. He has no idea where you are, and I told him I didn't either. I heard he went to talk to Jerry too.

Nausea curled in Lily's stomach and the bile started to rise. She forced herself to take deep breaths. *I'm an adult now. Pop can't hurt me anymore.* She had never doubted Pop would look for her. He needed her, after all, to do the things he didn't have the skills for. Or was just too lazy to do. Add in the money she took, and Pop would be really ticked off that he didn't know where she was.

Pop didn't like to have his plans disrupted.

But to talk to Jerry? Jerry had supported her plan to get out of Mississippi altogether and find someplace else to start over. He'd signed off on her paperwork with a smile, calling her the biggest success story to ever come out of the diversion program. Her probation officer had agreed. Her juvie records had been sealed, and she'd moved out of the halfway house and left town with a happy heart and a big sigh of relief.

Neither Jerry nor TJ would rat her out to Pop—not even if they did know where she was. They knew what kind of man he was. But if Pop was looking up her old friends and social workers that wasn't good.

Damn it. She didn't want to look over her shoulder anymore.

Lily closed the program and got several dollars in change from Judith, who told her she looked pale and asked if she needed to sit down. Lily took a minute to convince her she was fine, then left the library in a hurry. Two blocks away, she finally found a payphone and fed it quarters.

TJ answered on the third ring, but her voice sounded slurry and thick. *Damn.* If TJ was drinking again...

"It's Lily."

"Darlin'! How are you?"

"I'm good—really good. How are *you?*" For most people that would be an empty question, but in this situation it was so loaded Lily almost winced as she asked.

"Rollin' with the punches, darlin'."

Double damn. The only way TJ rolled with the punches was with a bottle in one hand. "Have you been to see Jerry?"

"Of course, and he's still just proud as a new daddy over you. Uses you as an example for all the newbies. You know, that's how I found out about your pop paying him a visit. That freaked me out."

"Well, I'm not worried about Pop. I am worried about *you,* though."

"Lily, darlin', I'm fine."

"You don't sound it."

"Oh, it's just the same ol', same ol'—ya know? Things around here never change."

That was what worried her.

TJ sighed. "But *your* last message…wow. You're really doing great. Sometimes I think I shoulda gone with you."

"You could have. And you could still leave, you know. Make a new start yourself."

"Nah. I'm good. Hey! I got news for you. Me and Roger are getting married."

Lily scrubbed a hand over her face in frustration. Roger's addictions were the very last thing TJ needed. Anything she tried to say about it, though, would either fall on deaf ears or alienate TJ. "Wow. I hope you guys are really happy together." The words left a horrible taste in her mouth.

"I'd invite you to the wedding, but I know you can't come."

"Yeah."

"Your pop's really angry, you know. He was cussing about not having a place to live when he got out."

Figured. "I wrote him and told him Sid had all his stuff in his basement."

"Yeah, but that doesn't change the fact the bank took the trailer. And he said you stole money from him."

That money was just as much mine as it was his. She would *not* feel one bit guilty for taking it. "Well, Pop will just have to deal with his own problems." *For once.*

"I promise I won't tell him nothin'. Not even that you called."

"I know. Thanks for the warning, though. And just stay away from Pop. You don't need to be involved."

"Don't you worry. Your pop ain't a problem for me."

"Take care of yourself, okay?"

"You, too, darlin'."

TJ hung up the phone, leaving Lily feeling desperately sad.

Lily fed another fistful of change into the phone. Jerry didn't answer, so she left a brief message, saying just that she was great, but that TJ could probably use checking in on. It was all she could do, really, and that sat heavy on her heart.

She finished her errands, but the satisfaction she'd been getting from a "new normal" escaped her now. Her new boots—tall enough to keep her feet dry no matter what trick Goose pulled—couldn't lift the cloud either.

She'd come so far, and the conversation with TJ underlined how just lucky she was to have made it out at all. On cue, she heard Jerry's voice. *"It's not luck. It takes hard work to change your life."* She couldn't save TJ—especially since TJ didn't want saving—but she'd managed to save herself. She should take a small measure of pride in that.

Even pulling into the long drive at Hill Chase didn't lift her spirits the way it normally did. The sight of the mansion, surrounded by rolling lawns, was picture-book perfect, as always, but the usual feeling she got at the sight was now all tangled up in Ethan, and it made her think of him and all that had happened when she really didn't want to deconstruct it all and ruin the memory.

Lily dropped off her stuff in her apartment, grabbed a water bottle, book and blanket, and headed for her favorite rock. She couldn't stay inside or else she'd just think, and she had way too much to think about today. She needed to escape for a little while.

She'd discovered the rock accidentally, but it was perfectly designed for leaning against while she read, and Lily tried to lose herself in a book.

Maybe she should have chosen a different book. The

romance novel she'd been so looking forward to reading was messing with her head. Around page three the hero morphed into Ethan, and nothing she did could shake the image. Ethan was a walking example of every hero ever written in a novel, and Lily could easily picture him as a Scottish laird—kilt and all.

And, with last night's memories still so fresh in her mind, the vivid descriptions on the page caused her breasts to feel tight and heavy and an aching heat to settle low in her belly.

Argh. She needed a horror novel, a thriller, even a tear-jerking memoir… Something *other* than a romance. Lily finally closed the book in frustration, leaned her head back and tried not to think about anything.

How long she watched the wispy clouds, she didn't know, but it didn't seem like very long before she heard hoofbeats. Horse and rider were easy to identify, and Lily wasn't sure if she was excited or nervous to see Ethan riding in her direction. With the afterglow faded away now, how was she supposed to face him? The shared intimacy of last night made an awkward gulf today—no matter how dispassionately she'd forced herself to examine it earlier.

Whether from nerves or hormones, her heart was pounding louder and faster than Tinker's hooves.

Ethan pulled Tinker to a stop and grinned at her. "Gloria told me I'd probably find you here. She sent you cookies."

The neutral topic of cookies helped a bit to ease into the idea of actually speaking to him. "Thanks." She held up her hands to catch the bag, but Ethan didn't toss it down. Instead, he dismounted and came to sit across from her on the blanket, opening the bag as he did. "I thought Gloria sent those for me," she teased.

"Surely you were going to share? After all, I did deliver them, and they're my all-time favorites." He was completely unrepentant as he took a big bite of a cookie. "What are you reading?"

Lily passed him the book, and Ethan's eyebrows went up as he read the title. "I wouldn't have thought you were the romance novel type."

"There's a type?" she challenged, taking a cookie for herself.

"Well..." He squirmed a little under her stare. "You just seem so practical."

"I can't be practical and like happy endings too?"

He shook his head. "There's a reason it's called fiction, you know."

"That's possibly the saddest, most cynical thing I've ever heard. I don't know if I should feel sorry for you or hate you on principle."

"Neither. I accept the world as it is. Realism is far better than optimism or cynicism."

"But it's possible to be realistic without losing your optimism and hope for the best." *And I would know.* But then, she realized, so should he. "Isn't that part of what politics is all about? Wanting to make things better even if you have to work with what you've got?"

Ethan seemed to consider her words for a second.

"Maybe. *If* that's why you go into politics. But I'm not involved in politics."

"But your father and—"

Ethan's face hardened. "I'm not my father," he snapped.

Lily realized she'd been right about Douglas Marshall and that he was obviously a sore spot with Ethan. But he seemed to catch himself quickly, and the lines in his face softened.

"Maybe that's where my cynicism comes from. I've spent my whole life surrounded by that system."

"I understand." And she did. Not exactly, granted, but close enough. She'd grown up in a system too—and a family business, in a way—and wasn't she doing much the same thing as Ethan by rejecting it for something else? "So, non-fiction for you, then? Just the facts?"

"Yes, ma'am." He reached for the bag of cookies again.

"How boring."

"Not at all. Choosing fact over fiction means I know how things are—not how I think they are or how they should be." Ethan stretched out on her blanket, stacking his hands behind his head. "Case in point—Lily Black."

Oh, no. "Excuse me?"

"You let everyone think you're shy because you keep to yourself. That's fiction, because I know you're not shy." Ethan's eyes roamed over her meaningfully and her skin heated. "You just don't want to talk to people.

That's fact. So, either you have some distrust of the world, or else you have something to hide."

She could hear the tease in his voice, but that didn't stop her stomach from dropping. She attempted to brush the statement off casually. "I just don't see the need to unload my life story on every person I meet, or get them more involved in my personal business than they need to be."

"I know for a fact you can't have too much to hide because you never would have passed the background check required for employment here."

Oh, dear God. Her mouth went dry and she nearly choked on the cookie.

"So," Ethan continued, "you either have intensely personal issues, or else you have a general distrust of people."

She took a long drink of water as she tried to figure out what to say, and then she tried not to sound defensive. "I may not implicitly trust everyone straight out of the gate, but there's a big difference between being a cautious and private person and being a distrustful and cynical one."

"You're saying that *I'm* distrustful and cynical?"

"Yes." *And it made her mad.* She kept her voice level. "And your need to see the world in black and white terms proves that. Not everything has a clear yes/no or true/false answer."

Ethan pushed up on to his elbow. "That depends on the questions you ask."

"And what if you don't like the answers you get?"

"It's all good as long as the answers are honest ones. Because then I have the facts I need to make a judgment."

Lily didn't know whether to be horrified or angry. "So you're judging me? I find that a bit offensive."

"Maybe 'judgment' wasn't the right word."

She needed out of this conversation. "*Honestly,* I'd agree."

Ethan smirked at her word choice. "But everyone has to make a call about people one way or the other. Even you."

"Oh, no, you're not painting me with that brush. I'm all about the gray area. I don't make snap judgments about anything or anyone—especially judgments based only on what people say."

"Three days ago you'd never laid eyes on me before, and last night—"

Great. Another place I didn't want this conversation to go. "Stop right there. If you want to talk about last night— Wait. Actually, let's not."

"Why not?"

She took a deep breath. "Because I get it. It was a one-off. You don't have to spell it out for me." She pushed to her feet and grabbed her stuff, causing Ethan to roll off into the grass as she tugged at the blanket. "It was great and all, but we can go right back to our lives now."

Ethan pushed to his feet as she started to walk away. "Can we back this conversation up a minute? What the hell are you talking about?"

"I'm not looking for a repeat of last night." She nearly choked on the words, because that *was* a lie. At least as far as her body was concerned. It was completely on board for Round Two. "In fact, I think we should back all the way up and return to a relationship with boundaries more appropriate to my position here at Hill Chase. Thank you for the cookies, Mr. Marshall. Enjoy the rest of your ride."

Ethan's jaw tensed, but she had no clue what that might mean—beyond the fact she'd hit a nerve somehow.

Thankfully, it wasn't a long walk back to her apartment, and even more thankfully, Ethan didn't say more or try to follow her.

Maybe she'd jumped ahead in this whole "new life" thing and needed to back up a few steps herself. She still had a lot of learning to do, and while her little crush on Ethan Marshall had seemed like a positive step, in retrospect she should have had better sense.

Live and learn and move on. Jerry used to amend that statement with, "Just don't be stupid at the same time," during group sessions. It was the unofficial motto of the diversion program, and had been tacked to the door of their house.

Maybe sleeping with Ethan wouldn't have to be filed under "stupid," but she'd learned something. She should be able to move on.

Ethan wasn't quite sure what had just happened. One minute they were having an impromptu picnic and an interesting conversation, but the next Lily was riled and storming off.

He whistled for Tinker, who trotted over immediately. He could easily catch up to Lily, but the angry set to her spine told him he should probably shouldn't. Maybe he should let her calm down a little first.

Not that he knew what he'd said to set her off.

Tinker had been waiting patiently, but now head-butted him to get his attention. Ethan put a foot in the stirrup, but noticed something on the ground a few feet away: Lily's book.

He shook his head as he went to rescue it. A woman who spoke of "appropriate relationships" while reading fairy tales. That was a new one. Of course he'd also never met a woman who didn't want to tell him every-thing about herself—in depth and in detail—either. She didn't think they were ready to share confidences, but they could, it seemed, have mind-blowing sex.

Lily was definitely different.

She was right about one thing: they'd skipped right over the ground rules. So setting some boundaries might be a good idea. *Where* exactly they were going to place those boundaries was up for discussion.

Even as prickly as Lily was, he was looking forward to that discussion. It should prove interesting…

Work and the Grands kept Ethan close to the house and busy longer than he planned, and even when he was finally able to make his escape the look Granddad sent his way was very telling.

Very little happened on the estate that Granddad didn't know about eventually, and even though he was an adult Ethan didn't like the idea Granddad might already know what was—or possibly wasn't—going on between him and Lily.

He laughed to himself as he climbed the stairs to Lily's. If Granddad knew, maybe he could fill *them* in on what was going on.

Lily called, "Come in!" to his knock, and he entered warily, unsure of the reception he'd get. Lily sat on the small sofa, feet curled under her and a book in her lap. The apartment was quiet, and dark except for the lamp that gave just enough light to read by.

Lily didn't look surprised to see him—or hostile, or pleased either, for that matter. Both her voice and face stayed neutral as she greeted him. "What brings you by?"

"I brought you this." He held out the book. "You dropped it earlier."

"Thank you. I went back to look for it, and when I couldn't find it figured I'd be paying the library to replace it."

"At least you had another one to read."

She moved the book in her lap to the side table and uncurled her legs from under her. The cutoffs she wore ended well above mid-thigh, giving him an almost complete view of the legs that had haunted him most of the day. "I checked out several from the library today."

The quiet room made the pauses in their conversation seem even more intense and drawn out, and despite his plans and intentions he couldn't think of a good way to broach the subject he'd come to discuss. Lily sat patiently, leaving the conversational ball in his court, and the silence spun out.

"I forget sometimes how quiet it gets out here at night."

"I like the silence."

She tucked her hair behind her ears, and he noticed it was damp from a shower. A deep breath and he could smell the lingering scent of her shampoo. The air was slightly moist too, meaning she'd only recently finished. An image sprang far too easily to mind, and that coupled with the fact her shirt was old and thin from washing— hiding nothing—had all of his blood rushing south.

When Lily spoke, he had to search for the topic of discussion. "Many years of noisy roommates will make you appreciate uninterrupted privacy and quiet."

That could have been a hint of some sort, but Lily was hard to read. The conversation was inane, but not overly stilted, so that was good. But she hadn't offered him a seat, either, so that wasn't promising. Not that there was much seating to choose from: on the couch next to her, which probably wouldn't be received well; her bed, which in his current state could prove disastrous to his higher brain functions; or one of the two small chairs at her table. This apartment was efficient and serviceable, but not exactly what he'd call comfortable.

"I should have called first—" *not that he would have* "—but you don't have a number listed on the contact sheet in Granddad's office."

"I don't have a phone." His shock must have shown on his face, because Lily laughed. "I know you find that hard to believe, but it's true. No computer either."

He looked around, as if he might see one or the other anyway. "How do you...?"

"I know you're tethered to yours like it provides oxygen, but plenty of people function just fine without either. I don't need to be in constant contact with the world."

He may not like the *constant* part all the time, but it was still nice to have the option. And, while it might seem like a stereotype, he'd never met a woman without a phone. "But in an emergency..."

That caused a smirk. "True emergencies are rare. And everyone else has a phone, anyway. *They* can call 911."

"How do you stay in touch with family? Your friends?"

She lifted a shoulder. "I don't have a lot of family, and I'm not particularly close to the kin I do have. I've lost touch with most of my old friends, and I've moved around so much recently that I haven't made a lot of—" Lily stopped herself. "If I do need to get in touch with someone back home, payphones and the postal service work just fine. However, I know how they work, and where to get one, so if I ever find myself needing a cell phone, I can get one."

Finding someone in this century under the age of fifty who wasn't digitally connected was rare enough to shock him, but Lily's admitted lack of family and friends went beyond shock into pity. At the same time, Lily didn't seem upset or in need of sympathy. In fact he would swear she sounded relieved. Or pleased, maybe. If she was really that alone in the world, she seemed fine with it.

"I do appreciate you returning the book." As she spoke, Lily reached for the book she'd laid down earlier.

Oh, no. He wasn't falling for that. He may have gotten off-track with their phone discussion—and he was beginning to think Lily changed the subject like that intentionally—but he wasn't leaving just yet. "That's not the only reason I came to see you."

Her shoulders tightened the tiniest bit, and she cleared her throat. "Oh? Did you need something else?" He could tell she was trying for a breezy, casual tone, but he could hear the tension underneath.

"Definitely." Since Lily wasn't offering him a seat, he took one of the chairs from the table. "We can start with discussing what happened last night and go from there."

Lily blew out her breath. "Why? Why do we have to discuss it?"

Just when he thought she couldn't surprise him more. *"Why?"*

"It just…*happened.* And it was nice—great, actually," she corrected at his look. "But, like I said, it didn't mean anything, and I certainly don't expect it to happen again. So there's really nothing to talk about."

Ethan took a deep breath to calm himself. Lily had to be the most frustrating women he'd ever met. "I don't agree."

"Then *you* talk." She folded her hands in her lap. "I've pretty much said all I have to say."

Now he wasn't sure where to start. He'd been on the receiving end of a we-need-to-talk conversation before, but never initiated one. It was disconcerting, to say the least—especially when Lily looked at him like...like... *that*. Like she was merely humoring him.

Don't lose your temper and say something you'll regret. Shaking some sense into her probably also wasn't the best idea, either, as tempting as it might be. But no other bright ideas were jumping to mind either.

"We're adults..."

Lily nodded.

"Reasonable adults...who happen to find each other... Ah, screw it."

Lily's eyes widened as he crossed the small distance separating them and hauled her to her feet. Her gasp of surprise was cut short as his mouth landed on hers. She didn't protest, though, and after the initial shock subsided returned the kiss with a hunger and fire that caused his blood to roar through his veins.

Her hair tangled between his fingers, and Lily rose on tiptoe to fit her body against his. She rubbed restlessly against him, and his hands slid to her waist to steady her.

"Ethan..." Lily pulled back the slightest bit and

took big gulps of air. "We probably shouldn't be doing this. Again."

"Tell me to stop and I will." He hoped he wouldn't have to test the truth of that statement. It might just kill him.

"I—I thought you wanted to talk." Her thumbs were caressing the muscles of his neck, causing small shivers to run over his skin.

"How about later?"

Lily's smile was gas on the fire. "Later works," she whispered against his lips, and began sliding his shirt up. He broke the kiss long enough to pull it over his head and then quickly removed hers as well.

Three steps backward and his calves hit the bed. He pulled Lily into his lap as he sat, then flipped her to her back and joined her on the mattress.

Lily couldn't catch her breath. Last night had been spontaneous, somehow outside of reality. *This* was very real. Ethan's mouth and hands were determined and thorough as they moved over her, removing the rest of her clothes and mapping every inch of her skin with a trail of fire. The frantic urgency of last night was gone— well, she still felt frantic and urgent, but for a different reason. Ethan was driving her right to the very edge with a deliberation that made her want to scream.

When he moved to the side of the bed and stood, her frustration took on a sharp edge. Watching Ethan watch her while he shucked the rest of his clothes only honed that edge.

But, *oh,* to finally have the heavy weight of his body

on hers, skin to skin... Any lingering doubts she had about the wisdom of her choice quickly vanished. For the first time in her life she was getting exactly what she wanted, exactly what she dreamed about. This was what Ethan was offering—nothing more, nothing less. And since it was all she could offer him, it was the closest to perfect she could ever hope to come.

CHAPTER SIX

"YOU'RE in an awfully good mood today. Who knew worming horses could make a woman smile?" Ray teased as they finished up with Spider.

Uh-oh. Maybe the humming had been a bit much. "It's a beautiful day. The birds are singing, the sun is shining, and no one spit worm paste back at me. What's not to be happy about?" Lily tried to shrug it off, but Ray had a knowing smile. *Watch yourself.*

But it was difficult—if not downright impossible—to keep the spring out of her step and the smile off her face. She had a secret—a happy one—even if it could probably get her fired.

The last couple of days had been…surreal. Well, maybe not surreal, but definitely not part of her normal reality. She and Ethan had never managed to have that full-on talk, but she felt confident that they had an understanding in place.

It is what it is. And that was *all* it was. She had asked Ethan for a bit of discretion. She did have to work here, and really didn't want to deal with the problems that would arise if rumor got around that she and Ethan were somehow involved. While Ethan had grumbled that "discretion" was just a nice word for "sneaking around," he had agreed it would be easier on them both.

So for the most part they went about their business as usual—hers in the stable, and his doing…whatever it was he did when he wasn't riding Tinker or hanging out in the stable. At least Ethan's presence in the stable wasn't unusual at all, so their paths crossed a lot. It wasn't long before she'd found herself looking forward to even the smallest interaction or conversation.

And he'd shown up at her door every night, not leaving last night until the sun was coming up this morning.

She was operating on very little sleep these days, but it was totally worth it. For lack of a better word, she was giddy. Like teenage-girl giddy. Thankfully, if anyone other than Ray had noticed, no one had said anything to her about her good mood. But she should probably tone it down.

Ray closed the door to Spider's stall. "Well, whatever's making you so happy, I'm glad to see it. Keep it up. It's good to see you smile."

"Thanks."

Ray went back to his office and Lily did a quick check of everyone's water. For a Saturday, it was a pretty calm day. While normally the entire Marshall family would descend on Hill Chase on the weekend, the fundraiser tonight had kept most of them in the city, and the few that had come out were staying busy up at the main house.

The fundraiser put a small damper on her good mood, since it meant she wouldn't be able to see Ethan tonight. He'd grumbled about the event a lot, coming up with a variety of reasons why he didn't want to attend, but she knew he would go just to please his grandparents, and for the sake of family harmony.

But something about the way Ethan grumbled told her she was missing a piece of the puzzle. He could claim that the people were shallow, or even trot out his general dislike of the inherent dishonesty of the political machine, but it simply didn't add up. There was another reason, one he wasn't sharing with her, and because of the nature of their "understanding" she didn't really feel comfortable asking.

She wasn't looking forward to tonight—both for herself and for Ethan. But for different reasons.

Speak of the devil. Like she'd conjured him with her thoughts, Ethan strode through the wide stable doors. Her pulse kicked up, and she wondered if she'd ever get past that reaction. He spotted her and smiled… *Probably not.*

She met him halfway and Ethan took hold of her elbow. "Got a minute?"

"Sure." She let him lead her out of the stable and around to the side of the building. When he started for the steps to her apartment, she stopped. "What's going on?"

"Come upstairs with me."

"*Now?* It's the middle of the day." She looked around to see if anyone was watching. "Are you insane? I've got work to do. I can't just disappear with you to… to…" She sputtered into silence as Ethan shook his head ruefully.

"Ah, Lily, as lovely as that thought is, that's not why I'm here. Come on."

She followed him up the stairs, and once inside her apartment Ethan pulled her into his arms and kissed her until she was boneless. "I thought you said…"

"I may not have time to seduce you properly and thoroughly, but I will *always* take advantage of the time I do have."

"So you brought me up here just to—?" She broke off as he shook his head and pointed to the large black bag stretched across the bed. "What's that?"

"Something for you to wear tonight."

It was an awfully big bag to contain some scrap of lacy lingerie…was Ethan even into that? Then the "tonight" part registered. "But the fundraiser is tonight."

"Exactly. I want you to come with me."

She'd never felt her heart jump and her stomach sink at the same time. "I don't think that's a good idea."

"Why not?"

"Do you want the entire list or just the top ten?"

Ethan leaned against her door and crossed his arms over his chest. "Start with one good reason."

She went with the easiest one. "It's a fundraiser, and I don't have any money to donate."

He shrugged that off. "But you're a constituent and likely voter. Plus, going to fancy parties is one of the few perks you get for knowing the right people."

But that didn't make *her* one of the right people, and that led nicely to her next objection. "Your grandmother will have a heart attack if you show up with me as your date."

"Nana's heart is just fine. She's tougher than she looks."

"That doesn't mean she'll be happy about it." *And I could get fired if she's not happy.*

"I can handle my grandmother. Any other arguments?"

Lily didn't want to have to go this far down her list. "I've never been to anything like that, and I have no idea how to act." It was embarrassing to admit that, but there weren't a lot of charm schools or cotillion clubs in Locken, Mississippi. Not that she would have been welcome or able to attend them anyway.

Ethan shrugged that away, too, like it was nothing, and Lily was tempted to smack him. "I've been doing this my whole life. The rules are simple. Make small talk." He ticked them off on his fingers as he spoke. "Be polite, but not too chatty. Chew with your mouth closed." She did smack him for that, but he laughed and continued. "Smile and nod. Drink enough to take the pain away, but not enough to act stupid and make the papers. It's not that much fun, but the food is usually pretty good." He grinned. "You're pretty and you're charming and you know my family. That goes a long way in D.C."

This was inviting disaster. "Ethan, I appreciate the invitation, but I can't."

"You have other plans?"

"No," she admitted.

"Then, please? We won't stay all night—just a couple of hours."

She was so torn. And not just because Ethan looked so adorable, either. Going to a fancy D.C. fundraising party was definitely crossing into Cinderella territory, and what girl didn't want to be Cinderella for one night? But she could make a huge fool of herself in front of all those important people, and that would embarrass Ethan *and* the entire Marshall family as well. She sighed. "So that's an appropriate dress?"

Ethan grinned at her indirect answer. "Dresses, plural. I've never done the fairy godmother thing before, so I called my cousin and had her pick a few options. You can wear whichever one you like best."

"What if they don't fit?"

"They will." He seemed so sure that Lily didn't doubt they would.

There were so many ways this could go horribly wrong. There was also a pretty good chance she or Ethan would really come to regret this. But she knew she'd regret it if she didn't go. She had enough regrets for the things she'd done. She didn't want any for the things she hadn't.

"What time should I be ready?"

"Fundraiser" was really a misnomer. If people really only wanted to support a candidate or platform they believed in, they could simply send a check. The purpose of a fundraiser wasn't to raise funds; it was to provide access for the donors, give them face-time to explain what they actually expected in return for their money. It was the oldest game in D.C., and Ethan didn't like to play it.

That was partly the reason he'd asked Lily to come. Escorting her gave him something to do—a reason to mingle *away* from those he didn't really want to mingle with. And she seemed to be having a good time. Her knowledge and love of horses had given her common ground with several people, and she was currently deep in conversation with two women her own age.

Of course Lily didn't know yet that one of them was the Vice-President's niece...

Brady came to stand beside him. Brady had been working the room when he arrived, so beyond a general greeting they hadn't had a chance to talk. "You brought *Lily?*"

"You already know the answer to that question. Is that a problem?"

"Not if you don't mind that the whole room is now buzzing with the news you're sleeping with one of the stablegirls."

"I simply brought a friend to an event. So what if she works for the Grands? Spin it properly, and suddenly we're 'in touch with the common man.'"

"The 'in touch' part is what I'm worried about. Surely you know how many promising careers have been killed by improper sexual relations with employees?"

Ethan laughed. "One, I don't want a political career, and two, she's not *my* employee."

"Splitting hairs is *my* job."

"As is overreacting, it seems."

Brady sighed. "Someone has to look at the bigger picture."

Not that again. "There is no picture, big or small. There's nothing to see here, and it's really no one else's business. End of story."

"You should know by now that's never the end of the story."

Good Lord. Brady had been sucked deep into the political machine. "You really need to get out of D.C., Bray. You're getting paranoid."

Brady shook his head. "It's not paranoia if they really are out to get you. This is politics. You know that."

This was a case in point why it sucked to be from a political family. The press believed everything was newsworthy and campaign fodder. "No, this is *not* politics. This is a private relationship between two consenting adults. The only person who might be allowed to get their panties in a twist is Nana, and that's only because she's Nana."

Brady took another sip of his drink. "Nana knows that best-case scenario is that we lose a good employee when it's all over."

"And worst-case?"

"I refuse to believe you're *that* naïve, Ethan. And if you are, five minutes of any cable news network should burst your bubble."

Brady had a point; he was blowing it all out of proportion, but it *was* a valid point. "There's so much going on with this campaign I don't think Lily and I will even pop on the radar."

"And you're absolutely sure Lily wants you only for your strong chin and sweet words?"

"What? You think I can't impress a woman on just my own merits?"

"Your 'merits' also include a sizable fortune and a powerful family. Hers don't."

Ethan shook his head. "When did you become such a classist snob?"

"It's not snobbery. When you date—"

"We're not sixteen, Bray. It's not *dating.*"

"Whatever you're doing, when you do it outside your social circle you run the risk of gold-diggers and social climbers. Not to mention tabloid coverage and potential lawsuits… It's a sad fact of life, but it's the number one reason why you don't get physically involved with random employees or people not in your same tax bracket. These things can come back to bite you on the ass."

"That's not untrue," Ethan conceded. "But, as you said, I'm not that naïve. I'm also not so naïve that I don't see Nana all over this conversation. She set you on me, didn't she?" He'd seen the look on Nana's face earlier.

Brady didn't even try to deny it. "There's a lot more here to consider than just your love-life. You have responsibilities, and—"

"Spare me, Bray. I wasn't born yesterday. I fully

understand where Nana—via you—is coming from. But you're jumping way ahead here."

"If you say so." Brady was a master of the scoff.

"I do. Lily and I are… Well, we're…"

"Oh, *that's* illuminating. I'm sure the press will quote you verbatim and the whole thing will blow right over."

"There's no need for sarcasm. It is what it is. Nothing more."

Brady met his eyes evenly. "Is Lily aware of that?"

"Yes."

"And this is not part of some plan to get a jab in at Dad?"

"I don't know. Is it working?"

"Be serious, Ethan."

"I can seriously tell you that Dad has nothing to do with any decision I made tonight. Or any decision I *ever* make, for that matter. I'm here because the Grands want me here. I brought Lily because I wanted to. I'll smile if the photo op appears, but you'll notice I've stayed on this side of the room."

"So has everyone else."

Ethan froze at the new voice and his fingers tightened around his glass. Mindful of Granddad's lecture, Ethan forced his face into a neutral smile for the sake of their audience, and greeted his father with a nod.

Douglas Marshall's hair was slightly darker, and streaked with gray, but Ethan felt like he was looking at himself twenty-five years from now. *That* didn't help his mood any. "You have a lot of people here you need to speak to. There's no need for me to take up any of that time."

"Just showing up isn't enough, Ethan."

"Oh, I'm very aware of that, and I've gone above and beyond to make sure I've spoken to all the *right* people. I've done my duty by my family."

His father bristled slightly at the insult. "I expected better from you."

"Why? I'm just following your example."

Douglas sucked in his breath, puffing up indignantly, and Brady stepped between them. "Don't start this here. Remember that you have an audience."

Ethan forced his shoulders down. "Of course. Don't want to cause embarrassment for the family."

"It's a little late for that, Ethan."

"Excuse me?"

"Your date. What *did* you think you'd accomplish by bringing her?" The disdain in his voice wasn't just about Lily, Ethan knew, but it had him seeing red anyway.

Ever the diplomat, Brady put his hand on Douglas's shoulder. "Lily's a lovely girl—very bright and interested in politics. I'm sure Ethan thought she'd enjoy seeing behind the scenes a little."

"No, I brought Lily because I wanted to. The fact it pisses you off is just a bonus."

"If you wanted to embarrass me by grabbing the tabloid headlines with your current flavor-of-the-week, you could have at least have found someone more appropriate, instead of some low-class—"

Brady cleared his throat sharply, cutting Douglas off. Ethan followed Brady's stare to see Lily standing a few feet away, her face pale. Under the gaze of all three men, a flush began to rise up her neck. She'd heard his father's braying.

Damn it. "Nice move, Senator. I think you just lost a couple of votes." He pushed past Brady and grabbed Lily's hand. "Let's go."

"I— It's all right."

"No, it's not."

"You can't just leave."

Damn straight he could. But hauling Lily out of here would only embarrass her more. "You're obviously not feeling well, so let's get you out of here." He looked at Brady, who nodded. Brady would handle it, making sure everyone got the official story of Lily's sudden illness.

His father just shrugged and walked away. Not that Ethan expected anything different.

The valet went to fetch his car as Ethan seethed and Lily looked uncomfortable. Unfortunately his condo still wasn't ready for habitation, so he had no choice but to make the drive back out to Hill Chase.

In the privacy of the car, he took Lily's hand. "I'm very sorry about that."

"Don't apologize. It's not untrue, or anything I'm not already aware of. I appreciate you taking me tonight, and all things considered I'm still not sorry I went." She smiled weakly. "But we both know I didn't belong there."

"That wasn't actually about you at all. That was my father taking cheap shots at me. You were just a handy weapon."

Lily nodded and was quiet. As the lights of D.C. faded behind them, she looked out the window and chewed on her lip. "My father's not a nice person either. At all." Her voice was barely above a whisper, and the words carried a heavy weight that hinted there was a lot more to that story. And that it was a painful story. "That's why I don't talk about him much. He's also part of the reason I left Mississippi."

No wonder she'd shut down and gotten angry when he asked her even simple questions about her past.

"I got away from it, though—came here and started over. I hate it because you can't do that. You can't get away from it. It's unfair." She took a deep breath and squeezed his hand. "Some people just suck, and there's nothing we can do about it."

His family was full of PhDs and MDs and every other degree available from the finest schools, and none of them got it. But Lily did. She didn't even know the full story and she got it. And she didn't try to analyze it or gloss it over with platitudes or flippant advice.

Ethan slammed on the brakes and pulled to the shoulder.

Surprised, Lily looked around. "What's wrong? Is everything—"

That was as far as she got before he stopped her words with a kiss.

"What was that for?" she asked with a small smile, several minutes later.

"Because people suck."

"Not all of them. Just some of them." She put a hand on his cheek. "*You* don't suck."

That felt like really high praise.

CHAPTER SEVEN

ETHAN'S condo was finished five days later. Ethan would be moving back to the city today. Lily had known it was coming, but general denial had been an easier route. Oh, Ethan hadn't said anything about the change in their situation, but Lily knew the happy interlude was coming to an end. Ethan had a life in D.C., an office that really needed him there more than just part-time... His visits to Hill Chase would be regulated back to the weekends.

Honestly, when she looked at their relationship critically it was really one built on convenience more than anything else.

Once she was no longer convenient, though...

She sighed as she ran the brush over Duke's shiny black coat. Ethan would find something—or someone—else to occupy his time and attention.

It just sucked. And it hurt a little too. But she was a big girl; she'd handled far worse than this and survived. She just needed to be happy she'd had the experience at all.

"There you are."

Lily jumped at the sound of Ethan's voice and nearly dropped the brush. He entered the stall, and in that relative privacy gave her a quick kiss.

"I'm about to head out."

What to say? "Drive carefully."

Ethan looked at her strangely, then shook his head. "I'm going to be covered up in meetings all day tomorrow, so I probably won't make it out here for Finn's birthday dinner tomorrow night."

"Sorry to hear that."

"Depending on what time you're done on Saturday, and what time Finn can get away, you can either ride in with him or drive yourself."

Huh? "To where?"

There was that strange look again. "My place. Finn's birthday party is Saturday night, remember? The limos will pick us up there."

Her insides did a little happy dance. "Oh, yeah. Sorry. I kinda got the days confused."

"So I'll see you Saturday?"

"Yeah."

Ethan gave her another quick kiss. "Bye." Outside Duke's stall, he stopped. "Oh, here." He tossed something at her, and she dropped Duke's brush to catch it.

"What's this?" *Stupid question.*

"It's a phone. You said you knew how they worked. I assumed you would recognize one." He grinned. "In respect to your objections, though, it's very basic— just voice and text. My numbers are programmed in already."

A warm glow spread through her insides. "Thanks."

"Now I can honestly say I'll call you later. Bye."

He left her standing there in Duke's stall, savoring that warm, happy feeling, even though she knew it had put a dopey smile on her face. Duke finally butted her to get her attention.

"Okay, okay." She put the phone in her pocket and retrieved Duke's brush. She'd been wrong. It wasn't the first time, but never had she been so glad to be so wrong.

At the same time, this meant she and Ethan were moving in to the unfamiliar territory of Something Else. She didn't know what that something was, but it meant she had to come to a decision. She'd been wrestling with it, but there weren't a lot of good options. Tell Ethan her whole dirty story and hope he understood? Would he hate her for who she used to be? He would be mad she hadn't told him already, but would he understand why she hadn't? Of course until this moment she'd been running on the assumption this wasn't going to last much longer anyway, so there wasn't really a reason to dig it up. But now…

It was a hell of a Catch-22.

He'd given her a phone. So *he* could call *her*.

As far as gifts went, it wasn't exactly the kind of present that others would call romantic. Not that she wanted chocolates or flowers. The atypical practicality of it only made it more… She sighed. There was that giddy feeling again. This time, though, there was something else underneath it—an unfamiliar feeling that made her both a little nauseous and slightly wobbly at the same time it made her happy.

This was new. And scary. And it had Ethan written all over it.

"Did Lily say how long she'd be?"

Finn shook his head as he stretched out and propped his feet on Ethan's new coffee table. "No, just that she was waiting on the vet to look at Biscuit's leg, and she'd leave as soon as she could." He paused to take a drink of his beer. "I hear *he* had a little fit when you showed up at the fundraiser with Lily?"

Ethan didn't need to ask who "he" was. "Oh, yeah."

Finn smirked. "Good."

"You two need to grow up." Brady came out of the kitchen carrying two beers and handed Ethan one.

Finn lifted his bottle in a mock toast. "Isn't that the purpose of birthdays? Proof of growing up?"

"You are living proof that calendar years mean nothing when it comes to actual maturity."

"Maturity has nothing to do with it. I get my kicks where I can." Finn held up a hand. "And don't start your 'greater good' lecture. I don't care."

Since Brady was obviously about to do just that, Ethan couldn't help but laugh.

"I don't owe that SOB anything. He's ignored me most of my life, so I'm just returning the favor."

"Consider yourself lucky," Ethan grumbled.

"I do," Finn said. "And if Lily irritates him, it just makes me like her all that much more. You know, if it wouldn't kill the Grands, I'd spill the whole story to anyone who would listen."

"And he knows it, too," Ethan said. "He's one lucky bastard."

"Tempting, though, isn't it?" Finn asked.

"But it wouldn't serve any real purpose," Brady cautioned. "Twenty-five-year-old gossip makes interesting internet chatter, but it won't move poll numbers or affect voters. Plenty of people are in unhappy and unfaithful marriages, and they don't drink themselves to death, so that looks more like Mom's weakness instead of something Dad did. There's no way to spin that into anything else. He's a popular politician—outside of this room, at least," Brady qualified, "and his supporters will attack her. Do you really want *that* to be how folks remember Mom?"

Ethan hated it when Brady got all reasonable. Finn stared into his drink.

But Brady wasn't done. "And, since we turned out pretty well, folks will assume *he* has to have done something right in the parenting department." Brady shrugged. "If you want to go whining to the press about what a horrible childhood you had because of him, that's all it will look like—poor little rich kids crying about how tough they had it. You won't find sympathy among the masses because your daddy didn't love you enough or pay enough attention to you. The backlash will land on you—and us," he added. "We're the ones who will have to wade through it over and over again for the rest of our lives. *And,* as you just said, it will kill the Grands. Do you really want that on your conscience?"

Finn sighed. "Do you have to be so rational? Could you pretend you're *not* the heir apparent and drop the official party line for one night? And just get mad? Consider it my birthday present."

Brady nodded. "Since I hadn't bought you anything anyway, that works out fine. He's a bastard."

Ethan laughed, and his phone vibrated at the same time. He read the message. "Lily's here and on her way up."

Brady's phone chimed a second later. "Good," Brady said, as he checked his. "The limos are here, too."

"Then it's party time," Finn said. "Finally."

Lily was having a very hard time acting nonchalant. She'd thought the fundraiser was difficult to pull off without looking like the hick she was, but this was some-how worse. The fundraiser had had a different feel to it: everyone at that party had been there to see and be seen, or to network, or curry favor. It had been superficial and very political. Completely false.

This was different. This was *actually* how the upper class lived.

She'd left everything she'd ever known behind the moment Ethan helped her into the limo, and though they'd only gone to DuPont Circle, it could just as well be another planet. The Planet of the Perfect People.

Some places might consider themselves exclusive, with their bouncers and velvet ropes, but those clubs were havens for the unwashed masses compared to *this* club. She'd never felt so out of place and obvious in her entire life.

Diem catered to the young elite of D.C.: it was trendy, yet classy, with a private entrance to frustrate the paparazzi and a closely monitored guestlist to ensure those partying were surrounded by only those of equal social and financial rank. Lily had fully expected to be turned away at the door for her lack of pedigree, but their entire party had been greeted pleasantly and escorted to a table to the left of the stage and the dance floor. While she felt like her low-class roots were as obvious as a bad bottle blond's, no one looked at her with scorn or disdain.

If anything, arriving as part of Finn Marshall's birthday party on Ethan Marshall's arm garnered her looks of envy from people who were far more used to being the envied.

Ethan leaned close as the first round of champagne was poured. "Have I told you how amazing you look tonight?"

He had, but the little shivers that ran over her skin had as much to do with the compliment as the feel of his breath on her neck and the husky tone of his voice. She turned sideways and adjusted the lapels of his jacket. "You look pretty amazing yourself." And he did. Yummy, in fact.

More importantly, Ethan's entire attitude was different from last week's fundraiser. There, he'd been on edge, withdrawn and tense. Tonight that was all gone, and it was easy to see he was enjoying himself. It made it easier for her to enjoy herself.

They were a relatively small party: the three Marshall siblings, a couple of cousins and her. But their numbers fluctuated as the club's other denizens made their way over to wish Finn a happy birthday, and Lily found herself surrounded by enough wealth and power to rival some small countries. Some were the children of senators and business moguls, but she also met lobbyists, Supreme Court clerks, congressional staffers… Everyone was a piece of the elite D.C. hierarchy. And it was just *normal* to them.

When the President's daughter arrived, and greeted all the Marshalls by name, Lily knew she'd moved into an entirely different solar system.

But her position as Ethan's date—clearly defined by the way his hand stayed either on her knee or around her shoulder—gifted her with automatic acceptance from the people who normally wouldn't have noticed her existence.

"You okay?" Ethan leaned close during a break in the music.

"Just a little overwhelmed," she confessed. At Ethan's confused look, she added, "All the people, the music…"

Confusion turned to concern. "Do we need to leave?"

"No. Not at all. I'm having a great time." In fact, Lily wanted to pinch herself.

"Are you sure?"

"Positive."

"Good." He grinned as he refilled her champagne flute. "I intend to get you tipsy and take advantage of you tonight."

Like she needed any alcohol for that. "Promises, promises…"

Ethan waggled his eyebrows and dropped a kiss on her bare shoulder. "I can promise you one thing…" His voice turned husky as he whispered several very delightful promises into her ear, causing her blood to heat and her nipples to tighten against the bodice of her dress.

Finn interrupted by dropping to the couch on her other side. "I'd tell you two to get a room, but you might actually do it, and it's far too early for anyone to leave."

Finn had the same good genes as his brothers—making him irresistible to most of the women in the club—but he was definitely the West Coast version of the Marshalls. Sun-bleached streaks highlighted his hair, and there was a casualness to his attitude that belied his blueblood background. Lily had worried that Finn might object to her tagging along to his celebration, but if he had any problem with her Finn hid it well behind that Hollywood-honed charm. It was impossible not to like him.

"Go away, Finn," Ethan growled good-naturedly. "This is a private conversation."

Finn leaned closer. "You're a very nice person, but you have deplorable taste in men. Ethan's almost as bad as Brady."

Brady was just a few feet away, chatting with one of his cousins, but turned when Finn said his name. "What about me?" Brady asked.

"Finn's hitting on my date and about to get hit in the mouth, birthday boy or not."

"But she's so pretty." Finn flashed a lady-killer smile at her. "Wanna dance, Lily?"

"You're an idiot," Ethan and Brady chorused.

Caught in the middle of the brotherly banter, all Lily could do was smile and sip at her drink.

She was in heaven.

Lily was a bit unstable on her feet as Ethan led her out of the club to the waiting limo. Her cheeks were flushed, but she wore an ear-to-ear grin. Her grip on his bicep tightened as she wobbled slightly on the skyscraper heels that made her legs look a mile long and emphasized the definition of her calf muscles.

As he helped her in, a worried crease formed on her brow. "Are you sure you don't want to stay with the others?"

"Positive," he assured her for the tenth time.

"Maybe I shouldn't have had that last glass of champagne."

"Feeling no pain, huh?"

"No pain. Just bliss." She slid closer on the seat as the driver pulled away from the club. "Tonight was so much fun. Thank you."

"I'm glad you enjoyed yourself." Lily's head dropped

against his shoulder and she sighed. "Uh-oh, someone's done for the night."

"Nope, not at all. Just enjoying the floaty feeling."

He was enjoying the feeling of Lily pressed against his side, and the lazy slide of her fingers over his chest as she toyed with the buttons on his shirt.

"I like your family."

It wasn't the first time she'd said that. He dropped a kiss on the top of her head. "And they like you."

Her hand paused, and he felt her frown against his chest. "I don't think Brady does."

"Oh, he does. But, sadly, Brady's social skills are often hindered by the stick up his—"

"Stop it. I know you don't mean that." But the reassurance must have helped, because her fingers went back to playing with his buttons.

"Oh, I mean it. It's his job."

"And Finn?"

"Finn's just Finn. You can't take anything he says seriously."

Lily looked up from the button she'd undone. "So he *doesn't* think I'm pretty?" She stuck her bottom lip out in an overdramatic pout.

He ran a finger over her lip. "Oh, he has excellent taste in women. It's the other ninety percent of the words that come out of his mouth that are garbage."

The pout morphed into a flirtatious grin. "So *you* think I'm pretty?"

"Someone's fishing for compliments."

Lily had opened three more buttons, and now slid

her hand inside his shirt. Her thumb brushed across his nipple, sending a jolt of desire through him, then her hand splayed open over his stomach. "I know it's a cliché, but you know what I've always wanted to do?"

Whatever it was, he was *very* interested. "What's that?"

He was briefly disappointed when Lily removed her hand and moved to the opposite seat. His mood quickly changed when, with a siren's smile, Lily reached one hand behind her back. The silky fabric of the dress loosened, and his blood rushed to his lap as Lily slid it slowly off her arms and down to her waist, unwrapping herself like a present.

A lift of her hips and small shimmy caused the dress to puddle around her ankles. A moment later, the dress landed in his lap, and Lily reclined across the leather seat wearing nothing but two scraps of black lace and those sexy shoes.

He barely had enough blood still circulating freely to think, but what few thoughts he could form only made the pressure against his zipper intensify. He couldn't decide whether to bury himself in her or prolong the luscious view.

It was a side to Lily he hadn't seen before, but her wicked smile told him how much she was enjoying this. He forced himself to stay put. Lily ran a finger over the top of her cleavage, and Ethan dug his fingers into his thighs to keep from snatching her into his lap.

"How long does it take to get back to your place?" The purr in her voice moved over him like a caress.

Ethan slammed a hand on to the speaker button.

"Yes, Mr. Marshall?"

"Circle the city for a while. We're in the mood to do a little sightseeing."

"Of course, Mr. Marshall."

Lily's lips twitched. "Which sights are you wanting to see?"

"Just one. The look on your face right before I make you scream."

He saw her bravado falter a little at his bluntness, but her lips parted and her breath kicked up a notch. He moved to her seat and draped her legs across his lap. She shivered as he slid a hand from ankle to hip. Goosebumps rose on her skin as he traced his tongue along the lacy edge of her bra. "How long do you think it will take me to get there?"

Lily's eyes widened, then closed in pleasure as he captured her nipple in his mouth.

It didn't take very long at all.

"You know, I didn't miss you at all while you were gone," Joyce grumbled as she eyeballed the latest stack of paperwork Ethan handed her. She was more than just an assistant, and she knew well how valuable she was to Ethan, which gave her a freedom of speech most other employees wouldn't dare exercise.

"You know you did."

She laid a stack of papers in front of him. "Sign here. Yes, for about five whole minutes—and then I discovered this amazing thing called A Life. I found it very intriguing. Here, too."

He scribbled his name. "Hey, I pay you good money not to have a life."

Joyce sighed. "You *so* need a hobby. And here."

"What did I just sign?" He scanned the pages.

"Your soul away."

"Oh, good. I was afraid it might be your raise."

"You're hysterical." Joyce restacked the papers neatly and slid them into a folder. "I do need you to look over the contract for the property in Chicago—and don't forget you have a conference call at two o'clock. And... Oh." She paused. "And it seems Senator Marshall is here to see you."

Ethan looked up to see his father standing in the doorway to his office. He had a smile on his face, which meant Ethan wasn't going to like the purpose of the visit.

At Ethan's nod, Joyce excused herself and shut the door on her way out. "We'll need to keep this brief. It's a busy day."

"Oh, this won't take long." Douglas made himself comfortable in one of the chairs across the desk from Ethan, and tapped a rolled-up sheaf of papers against his leg. "It's about your girlfriend."

"Just let it go. Lily isn't your business, and she's certainly not detrimental to the campaign, so—"

"She could be once the press finds everything out."

"Finds *what* out? That she works for Granddad? Big deal."

His father chuckled, which was never a good sign. "So you don't actually know? When I thought you'd started dating that woman just to spite me, I at least respected you for trying to score a point or two. The fact you don't actually know... Well, that's just pathetic. I'm rather disappointed in you."

"Well, it's not the first time, is it?" Ethan tossed the pen he was fiddling with onto the blotter and leaned back in his chair. "Let's just make this quick and easy. You're a lousy human being, and I'm a great disappointment to you because I refuse to think you're God. We've had this conversation before. Now, is there something else that brought you by, or are we done now?"

"You definitely inherited your brains from your mother." Douglas shook his head as he pushed to his feet. "I was going to go through this point by point, but I'll deny myself the pleasure." He tossed the papers he held onto Ethan's desk. "You've appeared in public with her twice. You can *hope* there are no pictures already heading to the press, but before there's a third time you should have a look at this."

On that cryptic note his father was gone, raising the question of what could be interesting enough to make the Senator take time out of his day to come to Ethan's office, and then not actually talk about it.

Not that Ethan minded the brevity. Any meeting—however brief—with his father was guaranteed to raise his blood pressure, and whatever was in this stack of papers was not going to help. Had their conversation been about anything other than Lily, he'd toss them in the trash unread. But he couldn't shake the strange feeling that had hold of him long enough to do so.

The top page was a memo, written by his father's chief of staff, referencing the investigation made into the background of Lily Ann Black.

The SOB had investigated Lily. The outrage that immediately rose was damped a bit by the fact his father wouldn't be crowing so much unless he'd found something. Something damning.

Did he really want to know?

Ethan flipped ahead, past Lily's employment application, her driving record, and the basic check they'd run on her before she was hired. The next page, though, took a moment to fully register, and once it did…

It was Lily's mugshot. Oh, she was much younger, probably still in her teens, and her hair was blond with bright red streaks. She wore way too much make-up, and it only accented the sullen look on her face. He barely recognized her.

She was just a kid. She could have been arrested for anything.

But as he flipped to the next page he realized it was far more accurate to say she'd been arrested for *everything.* And it wasn't just kid stuff, either, regardless of her juvenile offender status.

Hacking, conspiracy to defraud, forgery, petty larceny, fraud… *Sweet Jesus.* No wonder Lily had left Mississippi. The local judge probably wanted to throw her *under* the jail.

And Lily had never bothered to mention any of it.

The notation that her official records were sealed explained how Lily had passed the pre-employment background check at Hill Chase. It also showed that his father had pulled some major senatorial strings to get this information. Ethan's disgust at his father's misuse of power was quickly swamped by a far greater anger.

She'd been lying to him the whole damn time.

No wonder she kept to herself and didn't talk much. She wasn't shy or quiet. He'd been right that Lily just didn't want to talk.

And now he knew why.

Making it worse was the knowledge that her record—as extensive as it was—only showed what she'd been *caught* doing. The list of crimes she hadn't been arrested for was probably much longer.

God only knew what else she was hiding.

His next thought chilled him: what did she hope to gain by keeping all this hidden? People kept secrets for a reason, and it rarely ended up well or harmless. Brady's caution the night of the fundraiser weighed heavy. He came from a rich and powerful family; the background check that would have denied Lily a job was for their protection, and Lily had managed to circumvent that. Was he supposed to believe Lily had ended up working for them just by accident?

Lily certainly had a hell of an act going, and he'd swallowed it whole. Everything he knew about her was false.

And he'd fallen for it. Fallen for *her*.

Lily was nothing but a liar.

CHAPTER EIGHT

THE stable was busier today than usual; one of the "little kids," as Ethan called them, was hosting a slumber party this evening, and the draw of the horses was too strong for twelve ten-year-old girls to resist. Just keeping curious girls out from under the feet of the horses and the staff had Lily running.

This was on top of her usual workload—plus Duke had been cribbing again, this time even managing to find a loose fan wire and chew it to bits. The horse was lucky he hadn't electrocuted himself. The farrier was due back today, to shoe some more of the horses, and they were running a hand short. She ducked into the office to refill her water bottle and catch her breath.

She was busy, busy, busy, but she loved each and every item on her to-do list. She loved her job, her shiny new life and Ethan Marshall.

That was a new feeling—scary, yet exciting at the same time. It had been hard to admit it to herself, but once she did...

If she thought about it too much, though, she got

either moony-eyed or slightly overwhelmed, so she was trying very hard to just be in the moment. She couldn't allow herself to think about the past or the future, so just focusing on the moment was the best idea anyway.

The moment was more than enough for her right now. It was the closest to perfect she'd ever been, and Lily didn't know quite what to do with herself.

She shook her head to clear her thoughts of Ethan as she screwed the lid back on the bottle. When she heard the door open she turned, and her heart jumped to a happy, double-time thump when she saw Ethan standing there.

"Hey! This is a surprise. I didn't know you were coming by today."

Oddly, Ethan didn't return her greeting, and he didn't move other than to close the door behind him. That was when Lily noticed the crease between his eyebrows and the tense set of his jaw. Something was wrong. Very wrong. And while the sound of the lock sliding into place and Ethan's careful closing of the office blinds would normally send a rush through her, that odd look of *something* on his face caused concern instead.

"Is everything okay, Ethan?"

In a tone that made "grim" sound pleasant, Ethan said, "We need to talk."

She tried to lighten the mood a bit—she *needed* to, because Ethan was scaring her a little. "Isn't that supposed to be my line?" When he looked at her blankly, she added, "You know—I'm the girl? We're the ones who always need to talk?" The attempt at humor fell flat and died. Trying hard to ignore the bad feeling in her chest, Lily leaned against the desk and cleared her throat. "Okay, so what do we need to talk about?"

"This." Ethan pulled a rolled-up stack of papers out of his back pocket and tossed it to her.

She caught the papers and straightened them to see what they were. One glance caused her blood to freeze in her veins. "Wh-where did you get this?"

"The Jackson County Courthouse."

Now she knew what the *something* on his face was about. *Oh, dear God. Why now?* Her past rushed up to meet her, and she felt sick. Dizzy. She swallowed hard. "Those records are sealed."

He snorted. "Oh, they are—but that doesn't mean they don't still exist. You just have to know the right people. And we know everyone, as you've probably figured out by now." The ice in his voice belied the casual way Ethan crossed his arms across his chest and leaned against the wall. "Anything you'd like to say?"

Please don't hate me. She tried to stay rational and calm. "It was a long time ago."

Ethan's eyebrows went up in indignant surprise. "That's all you have to say for yourself? No denials or 'I-can-explain-this…'?"

"I can't deny it. It's all right there in black and white. Except for the possession charge. That was completely bogus." He didn't look convinced. She swallowed hard. "As for explanations… Well, there's not a lot to explain."

"Oh, I disagree."

Of course you do. "I was what you might call a troubled teen."

"Just 'troubled'?" Ethan's voice was controlled, but just barely. It didn't bode well. "Jeez, Lily, was there any law you *didn't* break?"

Don't even attempt to answer that. Stay calm. Reasonable. Focus on the present. "It was a long time ago, and I've straightened my life out now."

"And you just forgot to mention any of this to me?"

"It's not exactly something I'm going to bring up in casual conversation. I'm not proud of the things I did back then, and I don't like to talk about it."

"That's no excuse to hide the truth."

"That's why they seal juvie records, you know. So you can start over and not have to deal with it every single day of your adult life."

Anger etched lines in Ethan's face. "And when did you plan to tell me about that part of your life?"

"Never" seemed like a bad—however truthful—answer, but Ethan wasn't waiting on her to respond. He pushed off the wall and paced. "This is exactly the kind of thing I should know about *before* I'm seen in public with someone. When the papers get hold of the fact I've been dating an ex-con…"

"Is that the problem?" The small ray of hope that it was a press issue was soon crushed by a different realization. "You're ashamed to be seen in public with someone like me?" She felt sick.

Ethan's eyes were hot, but his words stayed cold. "You lied to me, Lily."

And he hated liars. The sick feeling grew worse. "No, I didn't. I just didn't tell you."

His jaw tightened. "I'm not going to split hairs with you. A lie of omission is still a lie, Lily."

"And you wonder why I didn't tell you? Look at how you're reacting…"

"I'm fully justified here. You're acting like you had a couple of unpaid parking tickets surface. This changes everything."

Her ensuing confusion at his words only made the sick feeling worse. "I don't understand. Are you upset that I have a past? Or that I didn't tell you about it?"

"Both," he snapped. "You're not the person I thought you were."

Tried, convicted—and, from the sound of his voice, soon to be executed. And he was completely wrong. *"That—"* she pointed to her rap sheet "—made me who I am today, but it doesn't mean I'm that person anymore."

"Nice verbal gymnastics. You should look into a political career."

He might as well have slapped her. "You don't believe people can change?"

"You just woke up one morning and decided to turn over a new leaf?" The sarcasm stung.

"Oh, I wish. It took a lot of hard work."

Ethan looked at her like she was something nasty on the stable floor. "I find it amusing that deciding *not* to break the law was hard work."

"It's harder than it sounds. Judge Harris gave me a chance." *Which is more than you're doing.*

"I don't see why."

God, she couldn't take much more of this derision. "Not everyone gets to grow up like you did, Ethan."

"Being poor does *not* give you an excuse to break the law."

She could feel the mud of her past trying to pull her under and suffocate her. *No, I've come too far.* "Your family business is politics—mine was hustling and cons and some other petty crimes. That's how we put food on the table."

"That doesn't make it less illegal."

Argh. "Growing up, I didn't even know what Pop was doing was illegal. It wasn't until Pop went away for the first time and the state put me in foster care that I learned what he was doing was wrong."

"And yet you launched your own career doing the same thing?"

"I worked for Pop. I didn't have much of a choice. And, honestly, I was so angry at the world by then—"

"Save it, Lily. Right and wrong are pretty easy to tell apart. You chose—"

Now she was angry. "I wish it was that easy. It's not. Some things just aren't that cut-and-dried."

"Yes, they are."

The pacing and his tone brought back bad memories of police stations and courtrooms, and hard questions from cops and attorneys that she'd rather forget. Her frustration bubbled over. "Look. I'm sorry if you're upset

I didn't disclose my entire past to you. When his last job went bad, Pop went to jail. Judge Harris said I deserved a chance to try making a life without Pop's influence, and I got put into a diversion program for four years instead. Successful completion meant my records would be sealed, and I could start over without any of that on my back. I did my part, and Judge Harris did his. As far as the law is concerned, none of it ever happened. So, no, I didn't tell you about it because it's none of your damn business."

"I disagree."

And she'd never get him to see it any other way. It was the last nail in the coffin, and tears burned her eyes. "I don't care."

"You can't pretend it never happened, Lily. You can't just escape your past like that."

"Maybe *you* can't, but I was doing just fine."

A muscle in Ethan's jaw began to twitch. "What the hell do you mean by that?"

"Some folks learn from their past. Grow beyond their mistakes. Overcome their issues. My father made me a criminal, but I'm clean now. What's your excuse?"

She didn't think it was possible for his jaw to get any tighter, but it did. She'd hit the exact nerve she'd aimed for. "Don't try to make this about me. *You're* the criminal and the liar. *You're* the one who's been dishonest in this relationship."

Lily was so angry her hands were shaking, but so nauseous she could barely speak. She still managed to meet his stare directly. "I've never lied to you. I've never been dishonest. At least not about what mattered," she added quietly.

Ethan missed her point, but she couldn't tell if it was intentional or not. "I don't believe you. And you're completely twisted if you think you can lie about your past and it doesn't matter either way."

"And you're a judgmental bastard to let it matter that much."

The silence that followed her outburst told her everything she needed to know. There was nothing she could say to change his mind or make him see her as anything other than the person she *used* to be.

She'd lost him. Hell, she'd lost him the moment he found out about her record. This whole conversation had been a waste of her breath.

So much for starting over. The thought that she'd never be able to escape... Bile rose in her throat.

She needed air.

Opening the door and walking out of that office was the hardest thing she'd ever done. Everything in the stable was exactly the same as it had been just a little while ago: horse-crazy little girls underfoot, the sounds of Duke destroying something else in his stall... The sights and sounds and smells hadn't changed. There was no indication her world had just collapsed around her, or that her heart and soul had just been ripped from her body.

The tears she'd been fighting back threatened to overflow. She had to concentrate on placing one foot in front of the other...

"Lily!" one of the hands called. "Can you—?"

One foot in front of the other. Don't stop walking.
"No, I can't." She had to get out of here before she broke down entirely. "Not right now."

She kept her chin up as she walked out the door into the sunshine, but the tears started flowing freely once she mounted the stairs to her apartment.

The pain inside her was enough to bring her to her knees, and she took deep breaths to steady herself.

I deserve this. It's karma kicking me in the teeth.

She'd hurt people—deceived them and used them. She deserved to pay for that, and karma was collecting on the debt. Deep down, she'd known the day would come when it would. But she'd never thought karma would be this harsh: giving her someone to love, then taking him away as part of her punishment.

But she couldn't deny it was fair. It hurt—so badly it was hard to breathe—but the pain was fairly earned.

Lily caught her breath and wiped her eyes. After the joy and hope and promise that had filled her recently, being kicked back down to zero to start over... It was depressing.

No. She wasn't completely at zero. She was just back where she'd been before Ethan crossed her path. She still had her job—or at least she *hoped* this wouldn't get her fired—she still had a place to live, and she was still a hell of a long way from Mississippi.

These were still good things. She just needed to focus on that. Whether she *could* with this hole in her chest was a different question. Getting over Ethan would be tough under any circumstances, but doing it here? At Hill Chase?

She never should have gotten involved with him in the first place.

"You were right, Bray."

The poker game had been abandoned hours ago, and Ethan and his brothers had gotten down to the real business of drinking. As always, they steered clear of politics and family, and stayed on safer, more entertaining, topics—like football, movies and cars. Usually women would have made that list too, but with the Lily debacle still fresh they'd ignored the proverbial elephant in the room.

As the night had progressed, it had got impossible not to bring it up, and the words escaped before Ethan really meant them to.

"Of course I was," Brady answered instantly. Then he leaned back in his chair and grinned. "About what?"

"Lily."

Brady's grin faded. "Yeah, sorry about that. But at least you found out before it was too late."

That was debatable. Lily's lies cut deep, and the betrayal hurt. He was used to being stabbed in the back, but he'd never had the knife in his chest before.

"The upside, though," Brady continued, "is that it was just a flash in the pan. The few blogs that got wind of you and Lily assumed she was just another of your flings and moved on without doing much digging. The damage has been minimal."

Minimal. Then why was he feeling the need to drink himself into oblivion again tonight? "Granddad let her keep her job. Said she's paid her debt to society and deserves her second chance."

"I still don't think that's a good idea," Brady grumbled. "He's too soft. How does he know she's really reformed? What if she steals something or…?"

Ethan shrugged. "Hell, I can't figure out why she'd even *want* to stay."

"Doesn't sound to me like she has anywhere else to go." Finn sighed and shook his head. "And you two call *me* the idiot? I can't believe we share the same gene pool."

Ethan turned in Finn's direction. "Got something to say, little brother?"

"Yeah. That you're both idiots." He pointed at Ethan. "Especially you. Brady gets a bit of a pass at the moment, since he's in campaign mode, but you? You're just an idiot."

"It's going to be hard to get by on your smile in Hollywood when you're missing a few teeth."

Finn smirked. "Aren't we touchy tonight? The truth really does hurt, doesn't it?"

Brady interrupted quickly. "Do you have something worthwhile to add to the conversation, Finn, or are you just talking to hear your head rattle?"

"You, Mr. Big Picture, can't look past Lily's record, and Mr. Honesty here is lying to himself. If you two don't kill me, the irony just might."

Brady looked at Ethan. "He's been in Hollywood so long he's forgotten how to see past the surface of anything."

"*Au contraire, mon frère.* Everyone comes to Hollywood to reinvent themselves. We expect it. Hell, we *respect* it." Finn leaned back and crossed his arms over his chest. "And, no matter how superficial you want to claim we are, Hollywood is the one place that will give you a second chance. And a third and a fourth, too, as long as you keep trying. It's people like you two who live in the past and pass judgment on everyone and everything."

Ethan rubbed a hand over his face. "Either I'm drunker than I thought, or else that might have actually made some sense."

Finn seemed to be enjoying this conversation. "I like Lily. And, honestly, what you've told me only makes me like her more. The fact she wants to stay at Hill Chase shows she's got guts, too. The only real black mark against her is that she got involved with *you*."

Ethan flipped his bottle cap at his brother in response.

Brady came to his defense. "That doesn't change the fact she lied to Ethan."

An eyebrow went up. "You asked her—point-blank and to her face—if she had a criminal past she was trying to forget?"

"Of course not. It never occurred to me I would need to."

"Then she didn't lie to you."

Ethan sighed. "It's not that clear-cut—"

"Coming from someone who sees the world in black and white absolutes, that's really funny."

Brady coughed. "For an idiot, he does have a point."

"It's bound to happen occasionally, I guess." Finn stood and stretched. "And now, since I have a very early flight tomorrow, I'll rest my case and go to bed." He sighed. "It's a shame it's so late. I really *like* being right."

Finn disappeared down the hall, and Brady went to get another round.

"He did make a good point," Ethan said quietly, mostly to himself, as he took the bottle Brady offered.

"I know. I'm surprised you see it, though."

That was what had been nagging at him underneath it all the last couple of days. He just hadn't been willing to acknowledge it. "A minute ago you were agreeing with me."

A wry smile tugged at Brady's mouth. "Just trying to look at the bigger picture."

"And what do you see? Beyond a couple of idiots?" he qualified.

Brady was quiet for a minute. "Do you love her?"

"What?"

"You heard me."

"I miss her," he hedged.

"Knowing your temper, you have some serious apologizing to do, then."

He *had* said some pretty horrible things in anger,

but that wouldn't be all he would have to apologize for. "You think I should?"

Brady seemed to understand. "If the alternative is you continuing to drink like this and being miserable, yeah. I think you should."

"And just pretend none of it ever happened?"

"Your part in this or Lily's?"

He thought for a minute. "Both."

"Lily came here looking for a second chance. Maybe she'll be willing to give *you* one. You've got to be damn sure, though, that there's nothing in her past you can't get over. And she's going to have to be willing to fully disclose, so that you—and we—can prepare for whatever kicks up because of it."

Ethan leaned his head back and closed his eyes. A couple of weeks ago Brady would have been stating the impossible. But that was before he met Lily.

And Lily had changed everything.

It was amazing how little anything changed in the wider world even as her own world fell apart. Sure, she heard some of the whispering behind her back, but people had always talked about her behind her back. She was used to that. At least this time she wasn't being scorned.

She'd feared she'd be outed, that her past would be laid out here for everyone to see, but amazingly the Marshalls had kept all of that information to themselves. Although everyone seemed to know that she and Ethan had been a thing, and now they weren't.

Their pity, though, wasn't much better than scorn.

And, while her heart hurt so bad it was all she could do to get out of bed in the morning, nothing else really changed at all. A meeting with the Senator in his study the day after Ethan confronted her had started off pretty uncomfortably, but he'd proved far more understanding—and forgiving—than his grandson. She still had her job, and everything had gone right back to the way it was.

Everything minus Ethan.

Well...almost, she thought as she let Goose drink from the river and looked out at the mountains. The contentment she'd found here before Ethan was missing now. That hurt too. But no one would be able to tell *that* just by looking at her.

She turned Goose back toward the stable and nudged him into a trot. As she got closer, Ray waved her over. He held Goose's halter as she dismounted.

Ray's eyebrows drew together. "You really should have told us, Lily."

Her heart squeezed painfully. Maybe she'd been totally wrong. "What's up?"

Ray wrapped one arm around her shoulders and hugged her. "Happy Birthday."

Confusion reigned. "It's not—"

"I've got a surprise for you." His grin spread across his ruddy face. "I'll take Goose—you just go right on over there into the stable."

Several of the other hands were standing around, with equally big smiles on their faces, and they burst into a very off-key version of "Happy Birthday." She could hear Ray's deep bass join in behind her.

Where had they all gotten the idea it was her birthday? And how to tell them they were wrong?

"Surprise, Lily!" someone called as she looked carefully around the door.

Her blood roared in her ears and she felt dizzy. *It can't be.* She closed her eyes, sure it had to be a hallucination, but when she opened them and he was still there she felt her stomach lurch and adrenaline pump through her veins.

Pop.

Here.

Holding balloons and a brightly wrapped box.

How had he found her? And how had he gotten onto the estate? She was supposed to be safe here. Questions and denials of the reality slammed into her, and the world got a little fuzzy around the edges.

Ray appeared at her side. "You okay?"

"I'm fine," she lied. "Just really surprised to see Pop." That much *was* true. She smiled to reassure Ray, and the crease between his brows smoothed out.

Pop strode forward, looking every inch the proud daddy, his smile probably fooling everyone except her. "Happy Birthday, little girl," he said loudly, wrapping her in a hug that made her skin crawl and her breakfast rise. Dropping his voice so only she could hear it, he added, "Smile, damn it."

Lily tried, but it felt wobbly.

"Go spend some time with your dad," Ray called. "We can handle this place for an hour or so."

Pop hauled her up against his side in what would look like a one-armed hug. His fingers dug painfully into her arm, but she kept that weak smile on her face. She'd have bruises tomorrow, but it wouldn't be the first time. At least she could be sure he wouldn't risk looking like anything other than a doting father in front of these people, so he'd probably keep his voice and fists under control.

Probably. Good Lord, she had to get Pop out of here. Now.

"What are you doing here?" she managed to choke out.

His reply was sharp, with no chance she'd misunderstand. "You owe me, girl, and I'm here to collect."

CHAPTER NINE

ETHAN wasn't sure if his headache was caused by Finn's attempt to drink him under the table last night, or by the amount of thinking he'd had to do afterwards. He took comfort, though, in the fact Finn had been feeling even more fragile than him as he left for the airport this morning, and that all that thinking had Ethan headed to Hill Chase this morning, to see if he could salvage anything with Lily.

He wasn't totally clear on what he was going to say, or how he was going to say it, but he *had* resigned himself to some groveling. There really wasn't a way to escape that, but he was man enough to admit it when he'd not only reacted badly but also let his temper lead him instead of his brain.

He scanned the paddocks as he passed, but Lily wasn't in any of them. He didn't see her as he entered the stable, either, and a look in the office produced only Ray.

"Where's Lily?"

"She's with her dad. He came to surprise her for her birthday."

The wrongness of that statement hit him from several directions. It wasn't Lily's birthday. And she didn't like her father. *Or so she claimed,* a little nasty voice said. He fought to keep his voice calm. "Do you know where they went? I'd like to meet him."

"They were headed for her apartment, last I saw."

Ethan nodded and closed the office door behind him. Outside, he climbed the steps to Lily's apartment and paused near the top. The door was closed, but the window next to the landing was open, and he could hear voices from inside: Lily's and a gravelly male one. The sound of his name stopped him in his tracks, and though he felt ridiculous doing it, he stepped closer to the window.

"But I'm not seeing Ethan anymore. He dumped me when he found out." Lily's voice sounded strained and on the edge of breaking.

"Get him back."

"It's not that simple, Pop."

"Any chance you're pregnant?"

Ethan's blood froze.

"*No!* God, no."

"Does he know that?"

"Pop, stop. I'll get you the money, okay?"

"You know the tabloids won't pay as much as his family would."

Good Lord. She wouldn't…

"But it will have to be enough. It's the best I can do."

"You could do better, girl. You know how."

"I'll think about it—work on it and see what I can come up with."

The chill in his veins was quickly warmed by growing anger at hearing Lily matter-of-factly discuss how best to sell him out for a quick buck. *The lying little…*

She'd been using him. Possibly all along. She'd said her family's "business" was grifting and cons; maybe that was why she'd come to Hill Chase in the first place. And he'd delivered exactly what she needed.

All her talk about turning over a new leaf and starting over had been just hot air. And he'd bought it. She'd looked him in the eye and lied, and he, in his stupidity, believed her.

Finn was right; he was an idiot.

"Ethan!" Ray called from the stable doors. "Did you find her?"

The voices inside fell silent, and Ethan hurried down the stairs. A moment later Lily's door opened and a middle-aged man with Lily's dark hair stepped out. Lily followed on his heels, her face pale and eyes wide. She stopped at the top of the stairs, watching her father. Although the sun was warm, she wrapped her arms around herself like she was cold, one hand rubbing the bicep of the other arm.

The man nodded and smiled as he passed them, and made his way to a beat-up pickup truck with Georgia plates. "Good to meet y'all. Take care of my girl," he called, and he got in and closed the door.

Once her father was halfway down the drive, Ethan heard a door slam and looked up to see that Lily had gone back inside. A second later, the window slammed shut as well.

Too late, Lily.

"That was a short visit," Ray mumbled.

Long enough, Ethan thought bitterly.

Part of him wanted to storm up those stairs and shake Lily senseless, but that would only give her more ammunition for whatever attack she was planning.

"I'll see you later, Ray. I need to go see Granddad."

Ray looked at him strangely, but nodded.

Damn it, he'd have to tell Granddad what was going on; he might not be so forgiving of Lily's past now. They should fire Lily immediately. But she was after money, and firing her might only give her grounds for a real lawsuit.

The number of ways this could go bad swam through his head. But it was good to have something to focus on beyond his own hurt and anger.

Their hands were rather tied when it came to managing and mitigating this. About the only thing he could really do was give Brady a heads-up to get the counter-spin machine warmed up and ready to go.

And the lawyers, too, he thought grimly.

Lily's hands were shaking so badly her toiletries kept slipping out of her grasp. She finally got them all in the bag and zipped it closed before setting it next to the door. She didn't own much, so packing went quickly. The three drawers' worth of clothes were easily scooped up and thrown into another duffle bag. She grabbed her boots out of the closet, but left the two beautiful dresses from Ethan hanging there.

Her breakfast still rolled around dangerously in her stomach, and she clenched her jaw against it. She didn't have the time to be sick. She had to get away from here. Far away. *Now.*

Exactly how Pop had found her was a puzzle for another day. All that mattered was Pop *had* found her. God, Lily felt seventeen again.

She'd sworn she'd *never* feel seventeen again.

Just then, the *how* hit her hard—and she wanted to smack herself for the stupidity. Hiding out at the Marshall estate had been a great idea; getting involved with one of their notorious grandsons…not so much. All it would have taken was one person to recognize her in a picture on some blog somewhere and… Why hadn't she thought *that* through?

Because I was too caught up in Ethan.

She didn't have time for self-flagellation right now. That could come later. The fact Pop knew she was here was enough to get her feet moving; him expecting her to use her relationship with Ethan to make money simply added speed.

She'd have said anything to Pop to get him to leave. Agreed to anything he wanted just to get him off the estate. But Pop would expect her to follow through.

She'd seen the dollar signs in his eyes as he'd looked around. Pop recognized what a big opportunity had landed in front of him, and he wouldn't let that opportunity pass.

Which meant Pop would never leave her alone now. This wasn't about her. It wasn't even about the money she'd taken from him anymore—even if she paid that back in full it wouldn't be enough to satisfy him. Not after he'd realized what a goldmine the Marshalls might be.

And Ethan probably knew. The look on his face... Dear God.

No. She couldn't think about Ethan at the moment. This wasn't about him anymore.

She couldn't stay here. Not now.

Lily looked around. That was pretty much everything. She grabbed the notepad off the fridge and wrote a quick note to Ray, thanking him for everything and quitting her job. That hurt, too, and tears pricked at her eyes as she took the key to the apartment off her keyring and sat it with the office keys on top of the note. *Damn Pop. Why'd they let him out of jail?*

Sliding a hand under the mattress, she retrieved the envelope containing her savings. It wasn't much, but it would get her away from Virginia. She'd figure out later where she was going.

She hoisted her bags over her shoulders and took one last look around the apartment. She'd been so happy here.

Lily eased her head out the door, looking to see if anyone was around. It would be safer to wait until tonight, but she just couldn't. For now, the coast was clear, and she bolted down the stairs, jumping the last three and running to the back of the stable where her car was parked.

Another minute and she was on the drive to the massive gates, and it was all she could do not to berate the guard at the gate for letting some stranger through simply because he claimed to be her father on a surprise birthday visit. Instead, she waved in a casual way and turned onto the highway like she was headed to town.

Several miles down the road, she pulled over to the shoulder and gave in to the tears she'd been holding back. When the sobs finally subsided there was no feeling of catharsis, only emptiness.

When she'd been in trouble before she'd always felt she had nothing really to lose. Now her chance at a normal life—at happiness—had been stripped away from her.

This was what hitting rock-bottom felt like.

Ethan was still in Granddad's study, divulging most of the sordid details and formulating a plan, when Ray knocked at the French doors leading to the patio a couple of hours later.

"Lily's gone," he said without preamble.

"What?"

"When she didn't come back to work I went to check on her. I found this note and her keys on the table. Her car is gone and the apartment is pretty much cleaned out."

Ethan took the note. It was very short—"thanks" and

"I quit"—and it wasn't even signed. He flipped it over like there might be more on the back.

Ray looked at him accusingly. "Did you say something to her?"

"I never spoke a word to her."

Granddad took the note and read it. "I have a feeling it has something to do with her father's visit."

That was the understatement of the year. Ethan hadn't expected the repercussions of that visit to hit quite so quickly—and certainly not like this.

Granddad rubbed a hand over his face. "Maybe you misunderstood the situation, son."

"I know what I heard." What it meant was up for grabs, though.

Ray looked puzzled. "If there's a situation…"

"I don't think it's going to involve us, Ray," Granddad said. "Sorry you'll be short-handed for a while, but I'll see about getting someone to replace Lily as soon as I can."

"I'm sorry she left." Ray shot Ethan a look, clearly blaming him for whatever had just happened. "Lily's a good kid and a hard worker. She's come a long way."

That got Ethan's attention. "What did she tell you?"

"Nothing specific. Just a feeling I got." He shook his head. "Maybe it was her father. She got a really strange look on her face when she first saw him, but she seemed happy enough after that."

"You said the apartment is pretty much cleaned out?" Granddad interrupted. "What did she leave behind?"

"A couple of things hanging in the closet. And her birthday present."

"It's *not* her birthday," Ethan gritted out. "Her father used that as an excuse to get on the estate."

Granddad put his hand on Ethan's arm. "Go see."

The red haze of anger and betrayal was rapidly giving way to something bordering on confusion. Lily's apartment looked much the same as it had when she'd lived there. Until this moment he hadn't realized how few personal touches Lily had put on the place.

As he'd expected, the things in the closet were the dresses he'd given her, but seeing them there felt like a slap. Why he felt that way, he had no idea.

Nothing about Lily—or his reactions to her, for that matter—made any damn sense at all.

A present sat on the bed, tethering two helium-filled balloons. Ray picked it up and handed it to him. "Look—she didn't even open it."

The package was light—too light—but he opened it anyway, confirming his suspicions. "It's empty."

Ray frowned. "Do you have any idea what the hell is going on?"

"I have a couple of theories." None of them made much sense, but he wasn't going to admit that.

"Maybe she'll call in a couple of days. At least to let us know where to send her last paycheck."

"I doubt it." Lily was on the run from something.

Just to test his theory, he pulled out his phone and stepped onto the porch. He scrolled to Lily's number and hit "call."

It rolled immediately to voicemail—a generic one, meaning she'd already deleted her personal greeting.

Lily not only wanted to run, she wanted to disappear.

Four days later, the phone he'd given Lily arrived back at his office, postmarked from a small town in southern Maryland.

There was no return address.

CHAPTER TEN

IT TOOK less than a week for Lily to drop off the face of the earth entirely. Three weeks after that, Ethan still had no idea where she'd gone. Lily had no credit cards, no bank accounts, no utilities listed in her name... Her driver's license and registration traced back only to her last known address and employer: Hill Chase.

And he knew for sure she wasn't there.

Wherever she was living, she was staying under the radar. He'd even had the investigator they kept on retainer quietly run her Social Security number, but no current employer popped up. If Lily was working, she was getting paid under the table.

And he was starting to worry.

While Brady had battened down the hatches in preparation for Lily selling some squalid and exaggerated story to the tabloids, all was quiet. Brady was still waiting and vigilant, but even he was now willing to admit the possibility that nothing would happen—after all, the longer Lily waited, the less interesting her story would be.

Ethan, though, was *sure* nothing would happen. But

no matter how many times he told Brady that, Brady was still choosing caution. He'd given up trying to convince him.

It had taken a bit of thinking—once he was no longer fogged by anger—to realize the look on Lily's face that day had been fear. He remembered the strain in her voice the night she'd told him her father wasn't a nice man and was part of the reason she'd left Mississippi. That was why she'd bolted from Hill Chase and disappeared. She was running from her father again.

Ethan was fully ready to admit he'd been wrong. That he'd overreacted and said ridiculous and horrible things. He was prepared to grovel, if necessary. But it was very hard to apologize when the intended recipient of the apology was nowhere to be found.

And, much to the frustration of their investigator, who said Lily was torpedoing his success rate, they had no idea where to start looking.

He scrolled through his email and returned a few phone calls, basically killing time until Brady finished up with the lobbyist meetings and was ready to grab some dinner. When Joyce buzzed him a little while later, he welcomed the interruption.

"Ethan, there's a Mr. Black here to see you." Joyce sounded cautious. "He doesn't have an appointment, but he says he's Lily's father, and that it's important that he speak with you."

Not having an appointment was Joyce-speak for "I have Security on standby to escort him from the building."

"Send him on in."

Joyce's shocked, "Okay..." spoke volumes. This would be interesting.

His second look at Oscar Black was even more tainted than his first, as their investigator had had much better luck in getting Oscar's entire story. *Those* records weren't sealed.

Other than in hair color, Lily must take after her mother. Where Lily was pale and slender, Oscar was olive-skinned and portly. And while Oscar was nicely dressed, looking much like an all-round average guy, Ethan could see the rough edges: the evidence of years of hard living and anger.

Something about Oscar set Ethan's teeth on edge immediately, but he couldn't put his finger on exactly what.

Without greeting or preamble, Oscar Black jumped right in. "Lily keeps telling me you're a good man, and I hope you really are."

Ethan wouldn't believe that Lily had gone back to her father. He leaned back and rudely propped his feet on his desk. "And why is that?"

"After the trouble you've gotten her in, I'm hoping you'll do the right thing." If there was a point between parental outrage and weasely wheedling, Oscar had hit it dead center.

"If Lily's in trouble, why hasn't *she* contacted me?"

"It's not that kind of trouble, if you get my meaning."

One strange perk of growing up in his family was that Ethan knew when someone was dancing around extortion and how to handle it. "Oh, I get your meaning. If Lily is pregnant with my child, I'll take full responsibility for them both."

Oscar turned an amusing color of green.

"In fact—" he pushed the phone across the desk "—call her right now and tell her that." Oscar hesitated, and Ethan sat back in his chair. "That's what I thought."

"You broke my baby's poor heart—"

"Save it."

The look that crossed Oscar's face nearly sent Ethan reeling. He'd seen the same look on his own father's face. The same scorn, the same anger when things didn't immediately go the way he planned. Oscar was Douglas Marshall without the money and social standing, working on the other side of the law and without a care for the "greater good."

Or anyone's good other than his own. And, from one report Ethan had, both men shared equally bad tempers—the only difference being the way they expressed them. His hands curled into fists, itching to take a swing.

Oscar was a small-time, small-town criminal, swimming in deep waters for the first time. Ethan felt like a shark sliding in as Oscar took too long to regroup and try a different tack.

"I know Lily's not involved with this. In fact, I doubt you have a damn clue where she even is right now. So, unless you have something else to talk to me about…"

Defeated and exposed, Oscar let his mask fall away

entirely, and Ethan's stomach turned over on Lily's behalf. No wonder Lily had been a "troubled teen." *This* was what Judge Harris had seen and why he'd cut Lily a deal. *Thank God*. He made a mental note to send a very large donation Judge Harris's way.

"Stupid girl landed in a damn goldmine and didn't have a clue what to do. Thought she was Cinder-freakin'-ella there for a little while—until you dumped her."

Ethan felt dirty just talking to the man. "I think you should take this as a hint that Lily no longer wants to—"

"I don't give a happy damn what that girl wants. Or what she does. But she owes me money, and I'll be damned if I'm going to just forget that."

"How much?" he snapped.

Oscar paused a second too long in his mental calculation of what Lily meant to Ethan versus the size of his checkbook. "Ten grand."

He couldn't do a thing about his own father, but maybe he could do something about Lily's. "I'll give you five. But that ends your relationship with Lily."

"She's my daughter."

"And for that she has my utmost sympathy." He hit the intercom on his desk. When Joyce answered, he kept eye contact with Oscar as he spoke. "Can you grab Frank Morgan and the blue box and come here?" Joyce sputtered her agreement, and he disconnected the call. "I'm not in the mood to bargain today. Five grand cash, right now, and you never get near Lily—or any member of *my* family, for that matter—again. And if you ever so much as come further north than Atlanta, I'll make sure you disappear without a trace. I suggest you take the deal."

Oscar's eyes narrowed. "Or what?"

"Or my Head of Security will sit on you while I call your parole officer and tell him you just attempted to blackmail the family of a sitting U.S. senator. You can finish out your last sentence and tack on at least another five years or so."

The door to his office opened and Joyce came in, carrying the cashbox from the safe. Frank Morgan stood next to the door, looking appropriately menacing.

"Make your choice."

Oscar was purple with anger. "The money," he snapped.

"I thought you'd see it that way." Ethan counted out the cash and handed it over. "Just remember that I'm a man of my word, and you *will* regret it if you cross me again. Frank, escort this...*person* from the premises and convince him he'd be wise to keep closer to the great state of Mississippi in the future."

"My pleasure, Mr. Marshall." Frank cracked his knuckles, and Oscar paled slightly as Frank followed him from the room.

Joyce closed the cashbox and smirked. "You just made Frank's day with that. He never gets to flex his muscles and play the intimidating bad guy anymore."

"I wish Frank would actually squash Oscar Black like the bug he is."

"I have a feeling Frank is hard-pressed at the moment

not to. Even his patience has its limits, and Lily's father is probably banging right up against them. If anyone could truly push Frank to violence, he might just be the one to do it."

"Hopefully Frank knows that I will get him the very best lawyers money can buy, should he be pushed over that edge today."

Joyce snorted. "I'm sure he does. Now, how do you want that money tagged in the books? 'Hush money' is not a line I wish to create."

Only Joyce… "I guess call it a gift."

"For Lily?" she clarified quietly.

"Yeah. It's one thing off her back."

"Too bad you have no way of telling her that. I'm sure she'd appreciate it."

Ethan didn't want Lily's appreciation. He wanted her current location.

Someone had to know where she was. It wasn't possible to just disappear. *Actually, it was,* he amended, and with Lily's background she probably knew how to do it. Working in his favor, though, was the fact that it was expensive, and he doubted Lily had the money to spend on a new identity. More importantly, it was also illegal.

And Lily wasn't a criminal.

Not anymore.

That gave him an idea.

I hate this dog. Lily rubbed the back of her hand where Pinky had snapped at her, glad to see it hadn't broken the skin this time. It went against the grain for her to hate any animal, but this spoiled, yappy, grumpy Pomeranian had earned her animosity.

"Look, furball, I don't like this any more than you do, but Mrs. Clarke wants your toenails pink, so give it up. I *will* win this battle."

Pinky the Pomeranian made her miss Goose, Tinker, Duke and the rest of the horses all the more. Cleveland made her miss rural Virginia. Her roommates, Karen and Paula, made her long for the quiet privacy of her little apartment over the stable offices at Hill Chase.

She was miserable. Lonely. She wanted her old life back. She wanted to go home—and home was Hill Chase.

And Ethan. Ethan was all tangled up in that misery, but she couldn't think about him. It hurt too much. She missed Ethan so badly it was a physical ache in her chest that kept her awake at night. She'd happily trade the rest of her wish list if she could just have Ethan. Not even for keeps; she'd settle for just a little while longer.

But all that was out of the question. Ethan had made his feelings very clear. In retrospect, she probably wouldn't have lasted at Hill Chase much longer anyway—with or without Pop showing up. He was too much a part of that, and being there *with* him when she couldn't *have* him would have been a special circle of hell designed just for her.

She adjusted Pinky, hooking an arm over his back

to hold him in place, and held the tiny paw still for a second coat of Pretty Pony Pink.

Pinky growled, his lips pulling back over tiny sharp teeth.

"I totally agree with your sentiment, but if you bite me again you're going to be a little furry football." Pinky cocked his head at her, and she relented. "Fine. No football. But I *will* shave you like a poodle. The other dogs will laugh."

Pinky made a little dog huffing sound.

"You know, you're not even a tenth of the size of Goose, but you're twice the trouble. God, I miss that horse."

"If it's any consolation, I think he misses you, too."

Pinky barked at the new voice, but Lily couldn't move. Adrenaline rushed through her, but her legs were frozen for some reason. *I'm hallucinating. Pinky gave me rabies and I've gone mad from it.* There had to be an explanation—one that made sense—because there was no reason at all for Ethan to be here. At the Pampered Pets Parlor. In Cleveland. Hell, he had no reason to even be in *Ohio*.

She carefully screwed the lid back on the bottle of polish and blew on Pinky's nails to dry them, but she was really stalling for time as she grasped for the right thing to say. Putting Pinky back into his carrier, where he growled in Ethan's general direction from complete safety, she cleared her throat. "This is definitely a surprise." She turned as she spoke, and seeing him there in the doorway made her heart hurt. Reality was even better than memory.

He was too casually dressed to be doing any business in the area, but the jeans, the boots and the UVA sweatshirt—that oddity stopped her briefly, since she knew he wasn't UVA—were as devastating on him as a tux. The sharp wind outside today had blown his hair around and reddened his cheeks. He looked adorable. Delicious. Heart-achingly wonderful.

"I would imagine it *is* a surprise. You, Lily, are a very tough lady to track down." Ethan stepped fully into the tiny grooming room and let the door swing shut behind him.

"Yet you managed to find me. Can I ask how?" *Because I'm not brave enough to ask why just yet.*

"It wasn't easy." He propped a hip on the grooming table. "We found a blog that had a picture of the two of us on it, and listed you by name."

"So *that's* how Pop knew I was at Hill Chase," she muttered.

"Probably. I contacted the blogger and found out who had identified you for him. Then I tracked *that* person down, and she told me she'd gone through that diversion program with you, and gave me the names of a few other people who were there at the same time. Their records aren't sealed like yours, so I eventually found your friend TJ who, after a ton of convincing on my part, told me you'd called her last week from a payphone in the 216 area code. Phone calls to every vet, pet shop, stable and kennel in the area finally paid off."

"That's an awful lot of trouble to go to." *And thankfully a hell of a lot more than Pop would be willing to do.* But that didn't really tell her why Ethan was here. She swallowed around the lump in her throat and asked the big question. "Can I ask why you did it?"

"We've been worried about you."

That was unexpected. "We?"

"Ray, Granddad, me." He smiled wryly. "Mainly me."

Her heart stuttered. "Well, as you can see, I'm fine."

"But you miss Goose?"

"Yeah, of course. I love those horses."

"Anything—or anyone—else you…um…miss?"

Ethan forced himself to ask the question because he was tired: tired of searching, tired of worrying, tired of beating around the bush. Lily did look fine—if a little morose and wary—and he didn't know whether to hug her in relief or strangle her for putting him through all of this.

"Honestly?" she asked.

"It would be nice."

Lily hesitated. "I really miss Hill Chase." *That* was certainly a slap to his ego. "I know I wasn't there for very long, but it felt like home. But once Pop found out I was there I just couldn't stay. He's not one to give up too easily, and he'd hound me."

"Your pop shouldn't be a problem for you anymore."

"Why not?"

"He made the mistake of coming to see *me*."

"Oh, God, I'm so sorry."

"Don't be. We had a nice chat. He tried to blackmail me—" Lily paled "—I paid him off and threatened his life and liberty if he ever came near either one of us again."

"You paid him off? For what? I don't—"

"There seemed to be a question of some money you owed him. Since I overheard your conversation that day—"

Lily groaned and sat. "That was the money I used to get to Virginia. It was as much mine as it was his. He just didn't see it that way."

"Well, you're clear now."

Her shoulders dropped a little. In relief, maybe, or something else? "I'll pay you back. It might take a while—"

"You think that's why I searched half the country for you and then flew to Cleveland? To hit you up for five thousand dollars?"

"Five?" Lily looked outraged now. "It was only three grand."

"Your Pop definitely has chutzpah, then. He asked for ten."

"Ten? That man has never had ten thousand dollars in his life," Lily muttered angrily.

"The money doesn't matter, Lily. The point is that your father shouldn't be a problem for you anymore. You can quit running."

"A blackmail attempt definitely violates his parole. You could have just had him arrested."

"That can still be arranged. Is that what you want?"

Lily's looked at him oddly. "Break the law, go to jail. It's pretty clear-cut, Ethan."

"I wasn't sure what *you'd* want me to do. He's your father—"

"Much to my dismay."

"Oh, you're preaching to the choir on that one, darlin'. But that just makes it all the more complicated."

Lily laughed. The sound warmed him.

"What's so funny?"

"You found the gray area."

"In all its many, many shades—thanks to you. Life used to be so much simpler."

"I don't know whether to congratulate you or apologize."

"I'm the one who owes you an apology. I overreacted and…" His entire carefully prepared speech escaped him now. "Well, people suck sometimes, remember?"

Lily's smile was small, but it was a smile nonetheless. "That they do. But after what you've done for me you've more than made up for it. Pop isn't brave enough to test you, and that lets me off the hook. It's a big relief. Thank you."

"I don't want your gratitude, Lily."

"*O-kay…*"

Damn it. He was going to have to grovel… "I want *you.*"

* * *

Just a second ago Lily wouldn't have thought it possible to be any more shocked than she already was. She was still reeling from everything Ethan had just laid on her, and now he went and topped the pile with that.

Her blood, which had run sluggish in her veins for weeks, suddenly began to circulate with a vengeance as her body took his statement at its most basic level of meaning.

Her brain, though, was misfiring. "You want me?"

"Yes."

"You mean like *now?* Here?" She looked around the dingy grooming room.

"Not *here,* necessarily, but, yes, now. And tomorrow, and for the next fifty years or so."

Pure joy poured like sunshine into her soul, but reality pulled the shades down quickly. She couldn't bring herself to fully accept what those words might mean. She needed a little time. Space. Possibly a strong drink or two.

"I think we should probably back up a little here." She stood and started to release the clasp on Pinky's cage, intending to end this conversation. "I, uh, get off work at four. We could go someplace and talk about—"

"Oh, for God's sake..." Ethan scooted off the table and grabbed her hand before she opened the cage.

Pinky growled and snapped.

"Look at me."

Lily forced her eyes up to Ethan's as his hands settled on her shoulders.

"I love you."

She closed her eyes and let the lovely feeling slide over her. It brought tears to her eyes, and the ache in her chest felt different. "Ethan…"

"I came all the way to freakin' *Cleveland* to tell you that. And to ask you to come home. With me."

If only it were that simple. "But my past is a disaster waiting to happen for you and your family. My record may be sealed, but I can't give people amnesia or make them not tell the press every last gory detail."

His hands were on her hair, smoothing it back from her face and tucking it behind her ears, and she fought the urge to curl into his hand like a kitten. "You think I care?"

"You *have* to care. I'll never live down my past."

"You don't have to live it down—because you lived through it and came out great on the other side. You said it yourself, you know. Your past made you who you are today, but it doesn't mean you're that person anymore." His lips brushed gently against hers. "I'm sorry you had to go through that hell first, but I love who you turned out to be."

"Really?"

"Honestly, truly and absolutely. No gray area at all."

"I love you." She was wrapping her arms around Ethan and feeling him pull her close…

She'd left Mississippi to make a fresh start at a new life.

But she'd never dreamed it could feel *this* good.

EPILOGUE

ALONE for the first time in days, Lily twirled in front of the cheval mirror and unsuccessfully tried to hold back the happy giggle. The elegance of the dress really required poise on her part, to complete the picture properly, but she was simply too giddy to even *try* to look poised today.

Not with *that* big dopey grin on her face.

It was nice to be back at Hill Chase, but Hill Chase didn't feel like home anymore. Home was with Ethan—and *where* that home happened to be didn't matter to her.

Instead of her tiny apartment over the stable, she now stayed in the mansion itself when they visited, climbing that amazing staircase to the family wing. Much to his grandmother's dismay, Ethan had shown her how to slide down the banister. And she'd gotten her chance to live out a movie moment when Ethan swept her into his arms and carried her up those stairs.

And, while she didn't get to work with the horses anymore, she could ride them to her heart's content.

Ethan had offered to buy her her own horse, but she was too attached to the others to want her own.

What amazed her the most, though, was that Ethan loved her. It had taken her a long time to really believe it, but now she did. And today—just minutes from now—she would marry him.

Cue dopey grin and happy giggle.

Of course there was plenty to rain on her parade if she'd let it. Starting with the two hundred people downstairs, most of whom thought Ethan was marrying way beneath him—which he was; she readily admitted that. But they'd come anyway, because an invite to a Marshall wedding was too coveted to pass up.

The irony was delicious.

Lily twirled one more time, and her phone rang. She had to dig it out of the bottom of a bag.

"Are you coming down or not?" Ethan's grumpy grumble actually warmed her.

Lily could hear the low rumble of the guests and the music of the string quartet in the background. "Is it time?"

"Past time. You're late for your own wedding."

"Your watch must be fast."

"Stalling, Lily Black? Getting cold feet?"

"Never. Just enjoying every moment of today."

"I promise it will get even better if you'll come on."

"Patience, Ethan. Are you in some kind of hurry?"

"Very much so." The truth and innuendo in his voice

sent happy shivers through her, and she nearly invited him up to her room.

"Then I'm on my way."

"Good."

On cue, there was a knock on the door and Leslie, their wedding planner, stuck her head in. "It's time."

"I told you I wasn't late. See you in a minute." She tossed the phone onto the bed. "I'm ready. Let's do this."

"You look beautiful," Leslie said. "Just like a princess."

"I feel like one."

The music changed as she stepped out onto the landing, and all eyes were on her. It didn't bother her, though, because Ethan stood at the foot of the staircase, handsome and perfect and wonderful enough to make her knees wobble and make her want to pinch herself to be sure this was all real.

Ethan loved her. Even after she'd confessed every sin of her past, every dark secret she'd wanted to forget, Ethan still loved her and wanted to marry her. More importantly, he'd helped heal her old wounds. She liked to think she was doing the same for him—healing the wounds of the past, and making a future where their pasts didn't hold sway.

Ethan had been wrong, and she loved reminding him of that. Reality and happy endings *were* possible outside of fiction.

Because she definitely felt like Cinderella.

And at the foot of this gleaming marble staircase was her happily-ever-after.

JUNE 2011
HARDBACK TITLES

ROMANCE

Passion and the Prince	Penny Jordan
For Duty's Sake	Lucy Monroe
Alessandro's Prize	Helen Bianchin
Mr and Mischief	Kate Hewitt
Wife in the Shadows	Sara Craven
The Brooding Stranger	Maggie Cox
An Inconvenient Obsession	Natasha Tate
The Girl He Never Noticed	Lindsay Armstrong
The Privileged and the Damned	Kimberly Lang
The Big Bad Boss	Susan Stephens
Her Desert Prince	Rebecca Winters
A Family for the Rugged Rancher	Donna Alward
The Boss's Surprise Son	Teresa Carpenter
Soldier on Her Doorstep	Soraya Lane
Ordinary Girl in a Tiara	Jessica Hart
Tempted by Trouble	Liz Fielding
Flirting with the Society Doctor	Janice Lynn
When One Night Isn't Enough	Wendy S Marcus

HISTORICAL

Ravished by the Rake	Louise Allen
The Rake of Hollowhurst Castle	Elizabeth Beacon
Bought for the Harem	Anne Herries
Slave Princess	Juliet Landon

MEDICAL™

Melting the Argentine Doctor's Heart	Meredith Webber
Small Town Marriage Miracle	Jennifer Taylor
St Piran's: Prince on the Children's Ward	Sarah Morgan
Harry St Clair: Rogue or Doctor?	Fiona McArthur

JUNE 2011
LARGE PRINT TITLES

ROMANCE

Flora's Defiance	Lynne Graham
The Reluctant Duke	Carole Mortimer
The Wedding Charade	Melanie Milburne
The Devil Wears Kolovsky	Carol Marinelli
The Nanny and the CEO	Rebecca Winters
Friends to Forever	Nikki Logan
Three Weddings and a Baby	Fiona Harper
The Last Summer of Being Single	Nina Harrington

HISTORICAL

Lady Arabella's Scandalous Marriage	Carole Mortimer
Dangerous Lord, Seductive Miss	Mary Brendan
Bound to the Barbarian	Carol Townend
The Shy Duchess	Amanda McCabe

MEDICAL™

St Piran's: The Wedding of The Year	Caroline Anderson
St Piran's: Rescuing Pregnant Cinderella	Carol Marinelli
A Christmas Knight	Kate Hardy
The Nurse Who Saved Christmas	Janice Lynn
The Midwife's Christmas Miracle	Jennifer Taylor
The Doctor's Society Sweetheart	Lucy Clark

JULY 2011
HARDBACK TITLES

ROMANCE

The Marriage Betrayal	Lynne Graham
The Ice Prince	Sandra Marton
Doukakis's Apprentice	Sarah Morgan
Surrender to the Past	Carole Mortimer
Heart of the Desert	Carol Marinelli
Reckless Night in Rio	Jennie Lucas
Her Impossible Boss	Cathy Williams
The Replacement Wife	Caitlin Crews
Dating and Other Dangers	Natalie Anderson
The S Before Ex	Mira Lyn Kelly
Her Outback Commander	Margaret Way
A Kiss to Seal the Deal	Nikki Logan
Baby on the Ranch	Susan Meier
The Army Ranger's Return	Soraya Lane
Girl in a Vintage Dress	Nicola Marsh
Rapunzel in New York	Nikki Logan
The Doctor & the Runaway Heiress	Marion Lennox
The Surgeon She Never Forgot	Melanie Milburne

HISTORICAL

Seduced by the Scoundrel	Louise Allen
Unmasking the Duke's Mistress	Margaret McPhee
To Catch a Husband…	Sarah Mallory
The Highlander's Redemption	Marguerite Kaye

MEDICAL™

The Playboy of Harley Street	Anne Fraser
Doctor on the Red Carpet	Anne Fraser
Just One Last Night…	Amy Andrews
Suddenly Single Sophie	Leonie Knight

JULY 2011
LARGE PRINT TITLES

ROMANCE

A Stormy Spanish Summer	Penny Jordan
Taming the Last St Claire	Carole Mortimer
Not a Marrying Man	Miranda Lee
The Far Side of Paradise	Robyn Donald
The Baby Swap Miracle	Caroline Anderson
Expecting Royal Twins!	Melissa McClone
To Dance with a Prince	Cara Colter
Molly Cooper's Dream Date	Barbara Hannay

HISTORICAL

Lady Folbroke's Delicious Deception	Christine Merrill
Breaking the Governess's Rules	Michelle Styles
Her Dark and Dangerous Lord	Anne Herries
How To Marry a Rake	Deb Marlowe

MEDICAL™

Sheikh, Children's Doctor...Husband	Meredith Webber
Six-Week Marriage Miracle	Jessica Matthews
Rescued by the Dreamy Doc	Amy Andrews
Navy Officer to Family Man	Emily Forbes
St Piran's: Italian Surgeon, Forbidden Bride	Margaret McDonagh
The Baby Who Stole the Doctor's Heart	Dianne Drake